THIS TATTOOED LAND

THIS TATTOOED LAND

DEREK PARKER

connorcourt
PUBLISHING

Published in 2014 by The Publisher's Apprentice
(An imprint of Connor Court Publishing Pty Ltd)

PO Box 224W
Ballarat VIC 3350
sales@connorcourt.com
www.connorcourt.com

ISBN: 9781925138276 (pbk.)

Cover design by Ian James

Printed in Australia

For those who hold fast, come what may.

CONTENTS

1. Corridor

Turner walked slowly along the curved, silent hallway.

So these are the corridors of power, he thought. There was a pungent, acrid smell in the air. *Must be the sheep.*

Most of the offices he passed were dark and empty, but in a few there were people. They were sitting at desks and writing on computers or pieces of paper. God knows what they were doing. Or what they thought they were doing.

He stopped and looked around. No-one. He took off his pack and reached into the compartment sewn into the bottom. He took the pistol out and put it into the pocket of his jacket. Glock 7-millimetre. Six bullets in the clip. No, he thought, only five. Well, that would be enough. More than enough.

He looked at his hands. They were dirty, even the blisters. The dust of a long road. Grey. Brown. Red.

He had thought that he might be scared when he got here. But he wasn't. Instead, he felt immensely calm. The weight of the gun was almost a comfort.

As he moved deeper into the building the signs of decay increased. The carpet, once green, was stained, worn through in places. Some of the office doors swung loose on broken hinges, and every now and then he passed faded, indecipherable graffiti on the walls.

Eventually, he came to a desk. There was a man in a faded uniform sitting there. His shirt said Security. He was playing a card game on an ancient computer. He looked up when Turner approached.

"Hi," he said. "Are you here for the tour?" A joke, presumably.

"No," said Turner. "I am here to see the Prime Minister."

Security grunted.

"What for?" he said.

Turner said nothing. In his pocket, he put his hand on the butt of the Glock. He eased the safety catch off.

Security grunted again. Then he pointed along the corridor. "Third door on the left," he said. "Right after the Director's office."

2. Dust

There was something vaguely pleasing about the *pocka-pocka-pocka* sound of the bicycle wheels turning. And the *kish* sound of the rubber on the wet road. It had rained last night, and the air was still cool. Good day for travelling.

Or maybe it was just good to be away from the farm. Not that it had been a particularly bad place. But eight years behind a fence was still eight years behind a fence. Should have been longer, he still had another two years on his sentence. Theoretically.

He wondered if he should have stayed. At least there was food from the fields and water from the river. *Here you will learn about the practical issues of sustainability*, he had been told by the supervisors when he had arrived. And surprisingly it had worked out that way. If a hundred men sweating in the sun and hacking away at the earth and carrying buckets of water, day in and day out, constituted sustainability. Well, thought Turner, maybe it did.

Food and water, that's what it came down to. So even when given the chance to walk away, no questions asked and no-one to ask them, a lot of the men had chosen to stay. That, plus the fact that they didn't have anything to go back to. Perhaps if you live for long enough on a patch of dirt you start to feel attached to it. The dust and the mud gets into your skin. Under it. Can't wash it out.

Not that leaving the farm was an easy thing to do. When he had arrived it had been in a bus, with twenty other men, mostly Recals. Over the next year, the bus had come several more times, delivering more men. The last time, it had wheezed to a halt a hundred metres from the gate. Out of petrol, maybe. Or something in it had broken. Or had just given up. So that batch of prisoners had had to walk in. Welcome to Sustainable Farm Q93, guys.

And from then on the bus had just sat there, slowly disintegrating. Someone had said it was a metaphor. No, someone else had said, it was a Toyota, it says so on the front. Turned out that the farm's chickens liked it, in any case.

But there had been some bicycles on the farm, old but serviceable. The supervisors had used them to ride around, check that everyone was doing what they were supposed to be doing. That was the idea, anyway. After a few years, the supervisors had got pretty sick of it. Instead, they spent a lot of their time in the Administration Office, the building that had been the original farmhouse of the property and was the only one with a fan. It had power from the farm's windmill.

That was where the bike had come from. Turner had asked the other guys if he could have it and everyone had said sure, no worries. Somebody had pointed out it was illegal to ride without a helmet. That had got a laugh from everyone.

So now he was riding through the countryside of rural Queensland. What used to be Queensland. With a few bottles of water and some food. Enough to last him for a while. The thin, grimy sleeping bag he had used for the past eight years. He was not sure where he was going. But it was good to be on the move, be in the open space, have different air around him.

According to the map he had found in Admin, the town of Roma wasn't far, going south. He had no idea what might be there. The only information about the rest of the country the farm had received was from new prisoners, and that had stopped with the bus, years ago.

The road linked up with a freeway, and he turned onto it. It was empty. He passed a sign. WRONG WAY GO BACK.

"Don't think so," he muttered to himself.

3. Population

He awoke with a shout. As he often did. Same dream. Didn't get any easier with repetition.

For a moment, staring into the darkness, he thought he was back on the farm. Then he remembered.

It was a roadside McDonalds, smashed up. Looked like it had been deserted for years. The big glass windows had been broken and the place was covered in graffiti. There was one huge slash of writing that had puzzled him, BDS THE LOT!!

There had been a storeroom in the back, untouched, so he had bedded down there. He had thought there might be some wood around for a fire, maybe some old furniture that could be broken up. But there was nothing. So dinner and breakfast – supplies he had brought from the farm – had been cold. Well, not the worst thing that had ever happened to him.

It was a couple of hours before he saw Roma on the horizon. Then there was a sign on the shoulder of the freeway, saying ROMA Population 6906. The number had been crossed out and 5200 had been written over it. That had been crossed out and replaced by 4550. Then 3000. That had been crossed out but there was nothing else. Whoever had been doing the counting had either given up or moved away.

On either side of the highway were crops. Or what had once been crops. Wheat and corn, mainly. But the fields were overgrown now, whatever had been planted there had climbed over the fences and was encroaching onto the road.

Up ahead, he could see something. A little group of people, six or seven, with a horse-drawn wagon. They were harvesting corn. They stopped when Turner rode up to them.

He introduced himself, and the leader of the little group introduced himself as Bowen.

"Going to Roma?" said Bowen.

"Yeah," said Turner. "Looking for some work, maybe."

"There's some work right here, if you want it," said Bowen. "We could use an extra hand, and you look like you know your way around a hoe." He mentioned a payment figure. It wasn't much, but it was the best offer Turner had had in eight years. So he took off his shirt and start picking corn.

They saw the tattoo on his arm.

"Done some time, eh?" said Bowen.

"Yeah," said Turner. "You want me to move on?"

Bowen shrugged. "I don't have a problem, and we haven't seen any Green Corps around here for a couple of months," he said.

"You from that farm up north a way?" said one of the women in the group.

"Was," said Turner. "Couple of weeks ago, we woke up and the supervisors had gone. They took the last working vehicle and left. Guess it had something to do with the fan. There was a windmill that had given us some power, ran a fan for the Admin building, few other things. Damn thing must have broken a dozen times. I'd fixed it but eventually there just weren't any more spare parts, and there's only so much you can do with duct tape. So no turbine. So no fan. So no supervisors. Least they left the gate open."

One of the men offered him a canteen of water. It was bitter.

"Bore water," said the man. "You get used to it."

They worked for several hours, until the baskets in the bag of the wagon were full. They started back to Roma, Turner riding on the wagon with the others, his bike on top of the corn.

After a while, they pulled into the main street of Roma. Bowen stopped the wagon in front of his store and they started to unload. Turner looked along the street. There were people – not many, but some – walking around, doing something or other. No cars. Some wagons, a few horses. A couple of broken-down trucks sat rusting under overgrown trees, parked forever. All the houses he could see had vegetable gardens in the front, people working in them with hoes and shovels.

He mentioned the population sign he had seen.

"It said 3000, did it?" said the guy that had given Bowen the water. "Bit out of date, then."

"Yeah, Roma used to be what they called a thriving regional community," said Bowen. "That was what the brochures from the Chamber of Commerce said, anyway. There was a lot of good farmland around here. Still is, I guess. But you can't do much farming without machinery, can you? Not on any sort of scale."

"And you can't run machinery without petrol," said someone else.

"We have enough to get by," said a woman. "Even if it means picking it by hand. We don't starve. That's something. Under the circumstances."

"Couple of years after the Declaration, people starting leaving," said Bowen. "Looking for work in the cities, I guess. Or looking to go somewhere else. Anywhere else." He pointed to a store across the road. "You look like you could use some new clothes, mate.

You probably shouldn't get around in the prison farm coveralls, it'll just attract the Green Corps. Go over there and get some new stuff for yourself. Clothes, shoes, a better pack than that one."

Turner looked at the store. The glass windows were plastered with posters of de Silva. "Uh, you haven't paid me yet," he said to Bowen.

"You don't have to pay there," said someone.

"What, it's a charity store?" said Turner.

"No, the people who used to run it upped and left a couple of years ago, said that anyone who wanted anything could have it," said Bowen. "No-one blamed them, their names were probably on a list somewhere. The Corps does love their lists. Used to, anyway."

Turner scratched his chin. "Odd," he said.

"Not really," said Bowen. "Pretty common story."

"Not one that I've heard," said Turner.

The others exchanged glances. Someone gave a short, sharp laugh.

"How long you been away, mate?" said Bowen.

"Too long," said Turner.

"Long enough for a lot of things to have changed," said the woman. "You know, you could stay if you want. Plenty of empty houses around here. You could just move into one, no-one would mind. I think you're the first person to come to Roma in while. All the traffic has been going the other way."

"I'm just passing through," said Turner. "Sorry."

4. Authority

Three days from Roma. He stopped to check the map. He had passed through a little village called Bala a while before, stopped and bought some fruit at a little market, with some of the money he had got from working for Bowen for a few days.

He was coming up to a ramshackle little house. There were two girls and a woman in the front yard, one of the kids playing on a swing attached to a tree. There was another swing but one of the ropes was broken.

He stopped. The girls and the woman looked at him.

"My husband is out the back," said the woman.

"Doubt it," said Turner. "But you don't need to worry."

"Huh," said the woman. "Well, I suppose we should offer you a drink. Of water, I mean."

"It's bore, doesn't taste very good," said one of the girls.

"That's alright, I'm used to it," said Turner. "If you like I can take a shot at repairing that swing. For the water."

So one of the girls brought out a bottle of water from the house and Turner repaired the swing.

"There you go," he said to the younger girl. "Swing away."

"Can't," said the girl. She pointed to her arm, and Turner saw that there was a grimy bandage there, above the elbow.

"Tattoo," said the woman. "Went wrong. Got infected. Over a year now. Won't heal."

"We've all got one," said the other girl. She pointed to her arm. It said EMITTER. He saw that the woman had the same.

"Huh," said Turner. "Haven't seen that one before." He pulled up the sleeve of his shirt and showed the girls.

"What does that mean?" said the older girl.

"It's short for something," he said. He turned to the woman. "What's the story?" he said to her.

In answer, the woman and the children led him to the back of the house. She pointed at something. It was a pile of coal, several metres high.

"There used to be a mine a couple of kilometres away," she said. "Not one of the big ones, just a little one for locals. When the coal mines were closed – that was the day after the Declaration – I guess they dumped some of the stuff that had been mined here. This place was empty then. We came along, we were looking for a place to live, the three of us, so we moved in. And we thought we could sell the coal. It gets cold around here in winter. So we did that for a while. Couple of years."

"And then the Green Corps came," said the older girl. "And we got our tattoos."

"It hurt," said the younger girl.

"Let me see it," said Turner. The mother unwrapped the bandage. The wound was red, inflamed. Not going to get better by itself. "This needs antibiotics," he said.

"Oh, right, well, I'll just run down to the chemist and get some then," said the woman.

Turner stared at her.

"Sorry," said the woman. "But there have been no antibiotics available for, I don't know, five years or more. No chemists, either. Not around here, anyway. Hard to run a business when you've got nothing to sell."

Turner scratched the stubble on his cheek.

"Got an idea," he said.

He got onto his bike and started back to Bala.

He arrived back at the little house several hours later. He had bought some fruit from the market and he gave it to the girls.

"Very nice of you," said the woman. "Hope you're not expecting anything in return. Can give you some coal if you want. That's about it."

"Don't need anything," said Turner. "Really, what I went to Bala for was this." He held up a paw-paw. It was very ripe. "You got something I can mash this up with?"

The woman led him into the kitchen of the house. She handed him a bowl and a fork.

While he was mashing the paw-paw, he said: "I haven't heard of anyone so young being marked before. She would have been, what, eight?"

"Yes, I mentioned that to them," said the woman. "Asked them what gave them the authority. They gave me this." She took a piece of paper from a drawer. It was faded, a copy of a copy of a copy.

It was a government regulation. Headed *Energy Production [Restrictions]*. Turner read it, struggling to decipher the unfamiliar language of officialdom. It said: … *all coal production, sale, and use prohibited … immediate and permanent … Green Corps empowered to use any means necessary to ensure prohibition … process identification to be initiated in all cases … by order and authority of Jonathan de Silva, Prime Minister …*

"So that's what they call it," said Turner. "Process identification."

"Guess so," said the woman.

Turner finished mashing the paw-paw. He handed the bowl to the woman.

"Let this sit for a few days," he said. "Ferment. Then put it on your girl's arm, like an ointment. It's an antiseptic. Not as good as an antibiotic but it should stop the inflammation, let the skin heal. It's better than nothing."

"Huh," said the woman. "Where did you learn about that?"

Turner shrugged. "I ... used to ... know someone," he said. "In the medical profession. Worked in a hospital. When the drugs started to run low they began to use things like this, she said. I suppose they wanted to save the manufactured medicines for the serious cases."

The woman nodded. She looked outside. It was getting dark.

"I suppose I owe you dinner," she said. "Not that I can provide much, just veges and an egg. And you can stay here tonight. In the front room. The girls and I will be in the back. Sorry if that sounds a bit rude ... but that's how it is."

"Yeah, I understand," said Turner. He looked at the page of writing that said process identification to be initiated in all cases. "Can I have this?" he said.

The woman shrugged. "Might as well," she said. "But why do you want it?"

"I'm ... not sure," said Turner.

5. Empty

He was close enough to see the faces. Battered, tired, scared. Some of the men wore old hats, some of the women had wrapped scarves around their heads to protect themselves from the sun.

Turner and the other cops were standing in a line, riot shields at the ready. He almost laughed at the absurdity of it. The little crowd of people standing in front of him were in no shape to stage a riot. Some of them could barely stand.

"Take this," said another cop. No, not a cop, the Green Corps squad leader.

Turner looked down at what he was holding.

He came awake with a start. In the semi-darkness, he looked down at his empty hands.

"Goddamn," he said to himself.

6. Map

He was standing by the roadside studying a map. He had found it in the wrecked McDonalds. It was a map of southern Queensland and New South Wales – the area that had once been known as southern Queensland and New South Wales – with all the McDonalds marked. It was full of cartoon faces and games for little kids but he had a feeling it might be useful.

He looked down the road. Brisbane was in that direction. He had lived there. Before.

He wondered if the little flat he had rented still existed. Maybe it did, maybe it didn't. From what he had seen in Roma, there didn't seem to be a housing shortage. In fact, there were far fewer people around then there used to be. From what Bowen had said, there was even a labour shortage, although the work to be done was mainly harvesting by hand or digging holes with a pick.

So perhaps no-one had moved into his place. What was once his place.

He had seen plenty of empty houses, either on the side of the freeway or in the little villages that had once offered food and petrol to travellers. He usually spent the night in one of them. It was better than sleeping in the open.

He looked again at the McDonalds map. The over-cheery face of that fellow with the orange hair stared at him.

He got onto the bike and started down the road. He had nowhere better to go.

7. Mall

It was a suburban shopping mall on the outskirts of the main part of the city. The doors, once automatic, were held open by a metal bar.

In the main atrium there was a little market, with people behind makeshift tables buying and selling various goods and items, mainly food.

Turner, glad of the shade, was wandering around. He still had a little money, and when he was buying some fruit he asked the vendor who was in charge. The woman had pointed to a short guy carrying a small chalkboard. Hammond, said the woman.

Turner went over to him and introduced himself. "You own this place?" he said.

Hammond gave a barking laugh. "Careful how you use that word," he said.

"Place?"

"Own. Some people don't like it. Property is theft, they say."

"Yeah, I've heard that line."

"But I help to organise things a bit. Someone's got to keep a record of who owes what to who, eh?" He held up the chalkboard. "And we live here. My family. They're all around somewhere, the wife and kids. There are a couple of other families that live here too."

"You live in a shopping mall?"

Hammond shrugged. "Good as anywhere," he said. "There's beds and stuff in the department store. For a while, there was a good stock of food in the supermarket. We had cooking equipment from the camping store. I used to be the manager of that one. That was good when we first moved in here but there's not much left now. Maybe only enough for another few months. Don't know what will happen then."

"But … doesn't someone else own all that?" said Turner.

"No-one that's around," said Hammond. "The mall used to be owned by a Jewish family, you see. They owned a string of them, some sort of trust arrangement, I think. As I understand it, they stuck around for as long as they could after the Declaration. But eventually the only choices they had was having it seized under the Property Security Act or being BDSed. So they got out, went … somewhere. Who knows where. Better than a tatt saying ZIONIST, eh?"

Turner nodded, although he did not really understand what Hammond meant.

"Me and the other people who had stores here kept it going for a couple of years after that. The small stores at least. The big ones just sort of stopped operating, no deliveries, no sales, no staff. Guess the guys at the top decided to quit as well. But we kept it going, place worked a bit like a real mall for a while. The blackouts were a problem but at least we had a bit of power of our own."

"Yeah, I saw the solar panels on the roof as I was coming in," said Turner. "That's what I wanted to talk to you about. They need some maintenance work, maybe? I used to be an electrician so I know my way around a wiring system."

Hammond laughed again. "Maintenance, in the sense of fixing?" he said. "They haven't operated for years. Let me tell you, it's pretty hard to operate a mall without lights or ventilation. That's why all we have is this." He gestured at the little market. "But if you can get them going, we can probably scratch up some cash for you. And you can have whatever is left from the stores here. I should probably tell you that that isn't much."

"Wouldn't mind a decent sleeping bag."

"I think there's a couple available."

"Deal."

After a stop at a disused hardware store to collect some tools, Hammond led Turner through the darkened stairwells to the roof, using battery-operated torches from the camping goods store. Turner took a look at the panels. Several of them were broken beyond repair but others looked as if they were serviceable.

"I'd say the problem is the inverters," said Turner, as he started to take the main terminal box apart. "Usually the first thing to go."

"You used to be an electrician, you say?" said Hammond.

"Before I was something else," said Turner. "And then something else after that."

"Haven't seen anyone who knows about this stuff for a while," said Hammond. "Most people who could do things like that went overseas. I've heard that Aussies re-built the entire electricity grid of Indonesia."

"Heard something like that once," said Turner.

It was a couple of hours later. Turner made his way back to the market and found Hammond.

"I've done what I could," he said. "Without new parts there's no way to bring the whole system back online. But I took bits from one section to use in another. Might give you thirty per cent of what you had before. Some lights, maybe enough to charge some laptops if you have them, maybe a refrigerator."

"Well, a glass of something is better than a bottle of nothing," said Hammond. He led Turner to the set of switches that controlled the overhead lights for the atrium. He pulled the lever.

Some of the lights flickered on. The people in the market looked up at them. They gave a ragged cheer.

"Son of a bitch," said Hammond. "Good goin', mate. That's worth a couple of bucks and a new sleeping bag, eh? But you can sleep in a decent bed tonight. Plenty in the store, at least. Mattress and clean sheets. Good enough?"

"Better than what I've had for a long while," said Turner.

But when Turner tried to sleep in a department-store bed, he found he couldn't. Too soft. He ended up sleeping on the floor.

Guess you get used to things, he thought.

Turner spent a few more days in the mall, tinkering with the power system and talking with the people who lived there. There was food, some from the supermarkets and some which people had grown and brought to the little market to sell, and water from a tank on the roof.

It was on the third day, when he was wandering through one of the abandoned areas of the mall, that he came across a smashed-up store. Looked like it had once sold chocolate or something, but that was years ago. Most of the big glass windows had been broken but one remained. It was covered with posters of Jonathan de Silva. His benign face stared out, the trace of a smile, visionary, as if imagining the good things to come. BUILDING A GREEN TOMORROW, said one of them. Turner had seen them before. Plenty of them.

Turner went into the store. Everything had been smashed, the counters, the furniture, everything, and the walls were covered with graffiti. Someone had had a good time.

There were more of the posters scattered about on the floor. He picked one up and looked at it. He looked at it for a long time. Then he folded it up and put it into his pack.

8. Tympanum

He was staring up at the top of the City Hall building. It was a series of relief sculptures in a triangular frame. A central figure spreading its arms to show the story of farmers growing things and workers making things to the world. Pointing the way to some sort of future for them. Sheltering them, maybe.

No, not sheltering them, pushing them, even as he watched he realised the central figure was pushing the others, pushing them down, pushing them away –

He snapped awake, sweating. In the translucent darkness of the store, he looked around. Nothing.

He looked down at his hands. They were shaking.

9. Secret

The door hung loose on its hinges, and he went in, leaning his bike against the wall in the place where the little table had once been. All the furniture, with the exception of one kitchen chair, had been removed years ago, and it gave the flat an echoing, ghostly quality.

He sat down on the chair and studied the dust motes drifting through the air.

He had not particularly liked the place when he had lived here. It had been necessary and convenient when he had been posted to Brisbane. You went where you were sent, if you didn't like it there were plenty of other people who would take the job.

Jean had visited from Newcastle whenever she could get away from the hospital but there had not been any suitable work for her in Brisbane. He wondered where she was right now.

He slapped his knees with his hands, telling himself to wake up. *No good muttering about things*, he told himself.

He went into the other room. One section of the faded carpet was loose, and he pulled it up. He counted the floorboards, almost surprised he could remember. It had, after all, been a long time. Three boards from the corner, four in.

With one of the screwdrivers in the toolkit he had got from the mall store, he prised the loose piece of board up. The package, wrapped in a cloth, was still in its compartment, untouched. As if it had been waiting for him. He took it out and peeled the cloth away.

Two hundred dollars in an envelope. A Glock 7-millimetre. Six in the clip.

You should feel ... something, he told himself. Anger, maybe. Regret. Apprehension.

He laid out the contents of his pack beside the cash and the gun. The poster. The copy of the Process Identification order. The little pack of tools. A torch. The McDonalds map.

You should feel ... something. Anything.

But he didn't.

Which means you have nothing to lose. Nothing left to lose.

He looked at the McDonalds map. On one side there was a list of Australian cities and the distances between them. Between Brisbane and Canberra was a distance of 1200 kilometres.

He picked up the gun, turning it over, extracting the clip and replacing it. He could remember the weight of it, the solidity. His hands remembered. His finger ran along the scratch on the butt, a legacy from the cop who had owned it before him.

Glocks always seemed small for their weight. You did not so much grip them as hold them, the way you held someone's hand. They knew what they were, what they were for. They did what they did without question, complaint, or pretensions of morality. You had to admire their honesty.

He looked at the poster. BUILDING A GREEN TOMORROW. By order and authority of Jonathan de Silva, Prime Minister ...

He thought of a piece of advice he had heard once, he wasn't really sure where. *If you can't do something smart, do something right.*

Turner did not know if the plan that was forming in his mind was either. But he felt he had to do something. Something. He owed it. To them.

It was the cut under the tongue that would not heal. It was the splinter in the eye that could not be removed.

His mother had said something that had stayed with him. Even now, long after she had gone, he could hear her voice saying it. *Pay your debts, cover your bills. When you go out, go out even.*

That was it, wasn't it?

He looked again at the map.

"1200 kilometres," he said aloud. "Long ride."

10. Pump

He spent some time staying in the little flat. During the day he would ride around the city, trying to understand what was going on. A large area near the river that had once been parkland had been converted to market gardens, and he got some work at one of the pumping stations that brought water from the river. Hard, mind-numbing work, but at least it gave him some extra cash and some baskets of food.

There were wind turbines and solar panels around, some operating, some not. One of the people at the pumping station told him that most houses got about two hours of power a day, less than last year. The power-sharing system was meant to operate on a roster basis but no-one considered it to be reliable.

"What's going on over there?" said Turner to Cheo, his pumping partner. He pointed at a large building where a team of people were doing something. "Construction?"

Cheo laughed. "Where you been, mate?" he said. "No, they're taking it apart, piece by piece. Recycling the stuff inside. Metal, wood, glass. It can be pretty lucrative if you're lucky. Wire is really valuable. I heard of one crew that started pulling some out of a big building and it just kept coming, they ended up with a couple of kilometres of the stuff."

"Don't people work in those buildings?" said Turner. "They used to, I remember it."

"What, you mean office work? All that ended years ago. Aside from the Green Corps going around and smashing up all the air-conditioners – even ripping them out of people's houses – there just wasn't any office work to do. All the big companies either closed up shop and went overseas or went under. I should know, I used to work in an office. Not far from here, just a couple of streets away. That building isn't there these days. Whole thing was taken down three, four years ago."

"What did you do?"

"I was an accountant. But not much point in knowing about business when there isn't much in the way of business, is there? So now I … pump. Sometimes. It's a break from hacking weeds and praying that it doesn't get too hot or too cold. Not much of one, though."

Turner looked around at the network of pipes leading to the gardens. The structure looked pretty ramshackle but was reasonably effective. Now he thought about it, it seemed that every square inch of open ground was taken up with something being grown. The only buildings that looked new were chicken coops, made from recycled sheets of metal and planks of wood. It was a universe away from what he remembered, a city of gleaming buildings and busy streets.

"Who organises all this?" he said to Cheo.

Cheo gestured to him that he should keep his voice down. "Not really anyone," he said. "There was a woman who did a lot of the set-up work, she had been a local councillor, I think. She brought a lot of things together, including the irrigation system. Pretty tough, pretty smart, saw what had to be done and told people how to do it."

"What happened to her?"

Cheo shrugged. "Word is that the Green Corps decided they didn't like her," he said. "People were starting to listen more to her than to them. One day she just wasn't around. I heard that she got a mark saying EXPLOITER and was sent off to one of the farms in the country. So now everyone is careful about looking as if they are organising things. It still happens, of course, but it's all done on the quiet, and on a small scale. Everyone keeps their heads down. I guess that that's what the Green Corps wanted."

Turner nodded. "Guess so," he said.

11. Steam

He was walking through the series of gardens in an area that had once been a park, running alongside what had once been a freeway, pushing his bike. He had finished his shift at the pumping station. He had a bit of money from the work, and he was thinking it was time for him to start moving.

He heard an unfamiliar sound, a clang of heavy pieces of metal making contact, and then a peculiar wheeze.

He turned to one of the people working in the garden nearby.

"Hey, mate," he said. "What's that?"

"You mean the train?" said the gardener. "The train station is just over that rise. They run every couple of days."

"Trains?" said Turner. "I thought there wouldn't be any electricity for them."

"You thought right," said the gardener. "The trains, both of them, are from the Historical and Preservation Society. Steam. Operate on wood and stuff from salvage. Not coal, of course. The Green Corps don't like them much, they say it's because of the emissions, but since they use them themselves I guess they can't do much about them. Wouldn't like to be one of the drivers though, myself, just in case the Green Corps has a change of heart. They do that."

"Huh," said Turner. "They ever go south, down the coast? Newcastle, maybe?"

"Only as far as Lismore, I think. Can't go any further than that, not since the floods."

"The what?"

"You know, the floods, must be five years ago now. Cut the highway and the rail line, no-one has repaired it. Don't know if they can't or just won't. These days, some things break, they stay broke."

"Floods," mused Turner. He thought of the 'education' sessions that he had sat through on the farm. Most of them consisted of the supervisors reading out chunks of reports from various government agencies or books from former politicians. He remembered one book which had said there would be a chronic shortage of water in Australia, the reservoirs would never be full, the rivers would be dry, drought would be the norm. "Didn't think that floods were supposed to happen," he said. "That's what some people said."

"Yeah, I recall all that stuff," said the gardener. "Whoever said it should have been here a few years back, when we had a little flood of our own. River came up. Not a big one, but where you're standing was under a couple of inches of water. I heard that the dams up in the mountains didn't have any power so the gates couldn't be operated."

Turner scratched his stubble. There was the sound of the train again.

"The train, does it take passengers?" he said.

"Sure," said the gardener. "Where're you going?"

"South," said Turner.

12. Stones

Fred Paterson Square. It had been called something else once ... what? He couldn't remember. And he couldn't remember when the government had re-named it.

But he remembered the looming sandstone tower of the City Hall, the strangely soft colour of the marble steps, the grass coming up between the concrete paving stones.

He remembered that some of the people had linked their arms. They had closed their eyes.

He came awake with a half-stifled shout. Sweating.

He lay back down, staring into the darkness.

He knew that he had been avoiding the Square. When he had walked by it, once, he had found himself looking in the other direction, as if there was something important happening over there.

Not that there would be anything to see if he went there. Not now. And he was not much of a one for symbolic pilgrimages.

Tomorrow, he thought, *I will leave. Long journey ahead.*

13. South

Much of the train station had been dismantled, the overhead wires taken down and the tracks pulled up. Turner wondered vaguely how anyone could recycle train-tracks, and where the engines and carriages had gone.

There was an open area, once a siding, where the train stood. There was a passenger carriage and a flat-bed wagon with a pile of metals pipes lashed to it.

Turner had his pack with all his supplies, which wasn't much. He had managed to sew a pocket into the bottom of the pack, large enough for the Glock. It meant that the gun could not be readily seen, although it would be found with any more than a cursory inspection. He had another bag, with some extra clothes and his sleeping kit, tied to the back of the bike.

He made his way to the engine, where there were two men sitting on the step. They were elderly men but still carried a good amount of muscle, the way that some men who have had a life dealing with machines do.

"You going down the coast?" Turner said.

"Nah, sorry, mate, we're doing the inland route, down towards Armidale," said one of the men. "We stop there and come back, that's as far as the line goes. Lismore is Thursday, the other train. You want a ticket? No charge for the bike."

Turner considered. "I guess I can wait until Thursday," he said.

The man shrugged. The two of them climbed into the engine and began to start it up. Turner began to walk back towards the gardens, pushing his bike.

And then he saw them. The olive uniforms of the Green Corps. There were four of them. Batons in holsters. They were walking along the track towards him.

He knew better than to run. He stopped until they reached him.

He heard the train exhale a breath of steam. It was getting ready to depart.

Two men and two women. Turner was surprised that their uniforms were dirty, a bit worn and battered. All the Green Corps members he had seen, before he went to the farm, had uniforms that were clean, even fastidious.

They looked at him. Turner kept his eyes down, not wanting to seem to challenge them.

"Where are you from?" said one of the women, at last. She looked like she was in charge of the squad. "You're not from around here, by the look of you."

Turner gave them the address of the little flat.

"Uh-huh," said the woman. "And before that?"

"Up near Roma. Came here for some work. I've been working at the pumping station the past few days. You can ask the other people there if you want to check."

"We'll do that," said the woman.

One of the others roughly pulled up Turner's sleeve, showing his tattoo.

"Looks like we've got a runner," he said.

"I did my time, learned my lesson," said Turner. "That's it."

"In my experience, Recals never learn much," said the woman. "By definition."

Turner said nothing.

One of the others said to him: "Let's see your carbon card."

"My what?" said Turner.

The four of them exchanged glances. "And that is enough of an offence right there," said one of them to the others, with a smile. "We should take a look at his stuff, in any case. Snap inspection, Recal."

From the corner of his eye, Turner saw the train began to move, slowly.

"Happy to show you," he said. "Not like I've got anything to hide." He put his hand on the bag attached to his bike, as if he was about to open it. The four Green Corps members seemed to relax, knowing they had won.

Turner lifted the bike and swung it around. It clipped into two of them, knocking them to the ground. He swung it again, and whacked into the other two. One of them cried out as he went down.

There was no time to get onto the bike. He hefted it onto his shoulder and started running for the train. It was moving, gathering speed.

He could see the Green Corps people picking themselves up and starting after him, pulling their batons out. If they caught him …

He reached the flat-bed wagon and swung the bike onto it. Now he was running alongside the track, looking for a way to hoist himself up. But the train was going faster, he had to run at full stretch to keep up.

He reached out for a low railing running along the side of the wagon, something that he might have been able to use as a handhold. He grasped it but the wagon was starting to outpace him. He stumbled, caught himself.

He looked ahead. There was a metal pole, close to the side of the track, zooming towards him. But if he let go of the wagon he was likely to fall, and then the Green Corps would be on him …

"Need a hand there, mate?" said a voice.

"Yeah, okay," panted Turner.

A man's hand reached down towards him. Someone on the wagon. Turner grabbed it with his free hand. He was pulled up, falling onto the wooden floor of the wagon just as the pole swung past. He glanced back. The Green Corps had stopped. They were already starting to walk back down the track, re-holstering their sticks. Maybe they thought they had moved him on, done their job. Shown an undesirable the door. Well, that was alright by him.

"They after you for any particular reason, or just general cantankerousness?" said the man on the wagon.

"Bit from column A, bit from column B," said Turner. He showed the man his mark.

The guy nodded. "Lot of that going around," he said. He introduced himself: Kozinski. Turner introduced himself.

"How come you're back here, not on the passenger carriage?" said Turner.

Kozinski gestured at the metal pipes tied to the wagon. "This stuff is mine," he said. "In the sense that I salvaged it, anyway. So I'm taking it down the line, see if I can find some customers. Done it before, it worked out alright. Used in latrines, mostly. Latrines and septic tanks, that's my business, although I never call it that. People still got to have a place to go, even if there's not a system, right? I was back here making sure this stuff was secure when they started off. Not a worry. They usually stop the train after an hour or so, the drivers have to change some points on the track. The passengers get out and have a stretch. We can go up and switch to the carriage then."

They retrieved Turner's bike and moved it to a more secure place on the wagon, and Kozinski used one of the extra ropes to tie it down. Then they sat against the pile of pipes, which offered some shelter against the slipstream. Kozinski offered Turner a drink from a canteen, which Turner gratefully accepted. Turner took some biscuits he had bought from a market stall from his pack and they shared them. They watched the suburbs slip past. Every house seemed to have a vegetable garden and a chicken coop, some had goats and even cows. In many of the yards there were people tending the plants or the animals.

Some houses had solar panels or roof-top windmills, although Turner couldn't tell if they were still working.

"Is this what people do now?" said Turner. "Grow food in their yards?"

"More or less," said Kozinski. "Most of the other jobs people used to have just sort of disappeared. Some people, like me, do some salvage and sell what they can. Or exchange it. Cash can be hard to come by, these days, if you're talking anything more than a few bucks. I can only really do that because I've got family at home who do the growing, so if I don't find any customers we don't all starve."

"Do most people have enough?" said Turner. "Enough to eat, I mean."

Kozinski stared at the yards as they went past. "Enough," he said eventually. "But everyone is always watching the sun and the rain. Funny, no-one used to think about that much. I don't know what they do in the southern states – what used to be the southern states, before all that stuff was abolished – where it gets cold in the winter. I suppose they burn whatever they can and just hope that the Green Corps doesn't notice.

"But, hey, on the plus side, obesity isn't a public health problem anymore, right?"

Turner was quiet for a while, thinking.

"The Green Corps guys wanted me to show them my carbon card," he said. "What's that?"

"Huh," said Kozinski. "Haven't heard of them for a bit, although I think I've still got one in my wallet somewhere. They were brought in, I don't know, six, maybe seven years ago. Look like a credit card, you remember them? Had a magnetic strip and everything. The idea was that every person had a certain allocation of carbon, like an account, and every time you did something that involved an emission or something you were supposed to swipe your card on a machine. If you went over a particular level you had to pay a fine."

"I remember that being talked about," said Turner. "Didn't know they actually did it."

"It never really worked," said Kozinski. "They didn't realise that the little machines you had to swipe your card on needed electricity, did they? And of course the whole system needed the Internet for the information to be collected, didn't it? So, yeah, the whole idea sort of collapsed as soon as it started. But you're still supposed to carry the damn card. If the Green Corps don't like the look of you, or want an excuse to bust you, they ask you for your carbon card. Not that they need an excuse."

Turner nodded. The train continued on, and in a while the suburbs were replaced by open countryside.

"I'm a bit concerned," said Turner, "that those guys back there will send a message on to the next town about me. So there'll be a squad waiting when we pull in."

Kozinski laughed. "And just how would they do that?" he said. "Carrier pigeon?"

Turner considered. He remembered that once every Green Corps squad had carried a Net-connected laptop, and every scrap of information was stored and passed around their network. They even had their own mobile phone system. But the ones he had left behind in Brisbane had had nothing like that, not that he had seen.

"I guess communication is a lot harder than it used to be, for everyone," he said. "In this case, that might not be a bad thing."

"You want to know what the most sophisticated communication device in the country is?" said Kozinski. "We're riding on it." He laughed again. "What, is there someone you want to communicate with? You got somebody?"

Turner was quiet for a while. Then he said: "No. No-one."

14. Run

Dear Jean

This will have to be quick. I've done something, well, I can't think of it as stupid but it's going to end with me being sent to jail, with a mark. You know how the Green Corps works, they'll track back to you and then you'll be in trouble, too. Wife of a former cop with a tatt, no future in it. So you have to get on a plane and go somewhere. Anywhere, but maybe your best bet is to try and get to your family in Wellington. I know that the NZ government announced it was closing its borders to Aussies a while ago but since you're half Kiwi you might be able to get in, and maybe they need good nurses.

But to get the exit permission you'll need to be able to show that you're not married to me. All it takes is for you to get a form from the Women's Commission, tick a box and hand it in and that's it, we'll be divorced. Take whatever money you can get out of the bank account, and then run, just run. Don't say anything to the people at the hospital, go and don't look back.

I'm going to give this letter to Corrigan, he said he'd do his best to get it to you.

Burn it as soon as you've read it.

All my love.

15. Rumours

About an hour out of Brisbane, the train stopped. The passengers got out of the carriage, and Turner and Kozinski jumped off the wagon and joined them. Turner walked along the line to the driver, who was struggling with the lever that moved the track.

"Changed your mind about Armidale, did you?" said the driver when he saw Turner.

"Something like that," said Turner. "So I need a ticket."

The driver wrote something on a scrap of paper and gave it to Turner, and Turner gave him the money.

The driver began to pull at the lever again. It was stuck. Turner gave him a hand, and eventually the lever moved, and the track jumped into place with a clang. The two of them started back to the train.

"You know," said the driver, "you could have just got into the carriage. Not told us, not paid. Not like we have a fancy ticket checking system or anything."

"Yeah, maybe," said Turner. "But you're doing something for me, I figure, so I should pay, since I've got a bit of cash in my pocket. You've still got to collect enough money to make this train a going proposition, right? Not like there aren't already enough problems, the last thing you need is people who think they deserve a free ride."

The old man nodded. "Thanks, anyway," he said. "And thanks for the help with that lever. I'm not as strong as I used to be."

"If you want to thank me," said Turner, "just keep it in mind.

And the next time there's someone who needs to get somewhere but can't pay, maybe you can just let it slide. Fair? After all, we've all got to help each other, I think."

"That we do," said the driver. "That we do." He climbed onto the train and Turner got into the passenger carriage.

He found Kozinski and sat down next to him. There was another three-person seat facing them, and a woman next to Turner. Maybe another dozen people in the carriage. As the train began to move again, a cool breeze came through the open windows. Fortunate, as there was a collection of pigs and goats tethered in the back, along with several wire cages with chickens clucking away.

"You on your way to Armidale?" said the man facing Turner to him.

"Yeah, but then continuing south," said Turner.

"What, Tamworth, Dubbo?"

"Further south than that."

You mean Orange, Goulburn? I've heard it gets a bit wild south of Dubbo. Gangs."

"No, that's wrong," said the woman sitting next to Turner. "That whole area is empty, down to Goulburn. Everyone just up and left. Went to Western Australia. That's what someone told me."

"Why would they go to Western Australia?" said Turner.

"I heard that WA seceded," said another person. "Became a separate country. The South Africans who were living there are running it now."

"You know what I heard?" said another person. "That Darwin has been sold. Lock, stock, and oil barrel. To Singapore. Which the people living there were pretty happy about. Well, they would be, wouldn't they?"

"That's like what happened in Cairns," said the man who had first spoken. "Most of it is a Chinese tourist resort now. Just for the Chinese, of course. That's what I heard. They have golf courses. And air-conditioning. Hey, you remember air-conditioning?"

Everyone suddenly thought about air-conditioning.

"Oh yeah," said the woman next to Turner, with a sigh.

"Probably why all those people from Bathurst moved to Perth," said someone.

Turner did not think that any of the stories sounded true. One thing you learned from being a cop is not to believe everything you heard. Too many things were just gossip piled on rumour, with a dose of speculation added. But everyone in the carriage seemed happy enough to trade tales about what they had heard, what someone had told them, what might or might not be the case.

After a while they stopped at a little town, so the engine could take on water and wood. Turner saw something, set back from the rail line. He realised it had once been a car sales yard. Hondas and Suzukis. But the place had been smashed up, and there were a dozen burned-out hulks of vehicles in the yard. On one of the big windows was graffiti: BDS THE LOT!!

"I've seen that before," he said to Kozinski, pointing to the scrawled message. "What does it mean?"

Someone in the little group gave a laugh. "You must have been away drovin', mate," he said.

"Something like that," said Turner.

"BDS," said Kozinski. "It stands for Boycott Divestment Sanction. Used to be something just for the far-outs, once upon a time. But after the Declaration it became government policy.

Although now I think about it I don't know if it was official policy or unofficial policy. Hard to tell with a lot of things like that."

"Started out as a protest against Israel, and against Jewish firms in Australia that sent money or goods there," said the man across from Turner. "The original idea of BDS was to try and get a better deal for the Palestinians."

"Well, that's what they said it was," said the woman next to Turner. "I was never so sure of that, myself."

"Anyway, after the Declaration it went from protests outside stores to smashing windows," said Kozinski. "Then breaking up the furniture. There were rumours that people who supported Israel were being tattooed. Don't know if that actually happened but it wouldn't have surprised me. Hell, they tattooed people for a lot of other things, didn't they? Still do."

Turner nodded.

"I remember reading about the Jews leaving," said the woman. "Planeloads at a time, special charter flights. That was before the government clamped down on it, of course. And then you had get a permission form. And leave any money you had behind."

"Yeah, I remember that too, the Jews lining up at the airports," said a man from another seat. "The BDSers were pretty happy. I remember them throwing things at the Jews as they left. And shouting things. Things that were … pretty awful. It was on television. That was when there was still television."

"Didn't the Green Corps do anything to stop them?" said Turner.

"The Green Corps," said someone, in a low voice, "were the ones doing the throwing. A lot of them, anyway. BDSers and Green Corps, they eventually became pretty much the same thing."

Turner scratched his stubble. "But how did protests against Israel end up with trashing a Honda dealership?" he said.

"I guess that once you get going with that sort of thing it's hard to stop, not that they wanted to stop," said Kozinski. "Like the tatts, a natural progression. They started tattooing people for being climate change sceptics but soon decided it was good for anything they didn't like. BDS was the same sort of thing. They figured that if they could get rid of the Jews the same tactics could be used in other ways. The next target was ... I forget, was it the Japanese or the Americans?"

"The Japanese," said the woman. "Over ... uh, I think it had something to do with whaling."

"And the Americans came after that," said the man in the other seat. "Not sure why. I suppose it was for being American."

"And then the Brits," said the man opposite Turner. "For 'their history of oppressive colonialism', the BDSers said. Or maybe it was because they started beating us at the cricket. And who was next?"

"The Chinese and the Indians were at the same time, pretty well," said the woman. "Treatment of gay people in their countries, as I recall. That actually didn't matter that much, all of the Chinese and Indian people who had been living in Australia left straight after the Jews, if they had somewhere they could go. Guess they saw what was coming down the road at them."

"One way or another, it became BDS The Lot," said Kozinski. "A catch-all. You can always find something to complain about, if you look hard enough."

"Did it do anything?" said Turner. "Did Israel change its policies on the Palestinians, did the Japanese stop whaling, anything like that?"

Everybody laughed. "I think you might be missing the point, mate," said someone to him.

At that moment, the train passed another burned-out, BDSed building. Turner stared at it as it slid by.

"Which is?" he said.

"That some people just like smashing things," said the woman.

Turner was quiet for a while, turning it over in his mind. Then he said: "Yeah. Some people do."

16. Facility

Turner slowly drifted back to consciousness.

"G'day," said a voice. "Glad to see you're still alive. You had me worried there."

"Not the first time I've been tasered," said Turner, rubbing the spot on his chest where the weapon had hit him. "Where am I?"

"Tamworth Community Short-term Correctional Facility," said the voice. "Jail, in a word."

Turner sat up. Yes, it was a jail cell, alright. Bars and everything.

The man who belonged to the voice handed him a plastic tumbler of water. Turner took it and drank. He introduced himself. It was just the two of them in the cell, no-one else around. Turner gave an inward sigh of relief at that.

"And I'm Callister," said the man. He was a portly, balding fellow, with heavy glasses that made him look strangely unfocused. "Pleased to meet you, sorry it isn't under better circumstances," he said.

"You wouldn't happen to know where my backpack is, would you?" said Turner.

"Sorry, mate, no, you didn't have it when they dragged you in and dumped you on the bunk. Something important in it?"

"Sort of."

"So – I've always wanted to say this – what are you in for?"

Turner considered. "For being an arsehole, I think," he said. "What about you?"

Callister shrugged. "I collected weather data," he said. "Rainfall and temperatures."

"Huh?" said Turner. "That's a crime, now?"

"Apparently so," said Callister. "Although something doesn't have to be a crime for it to land you in jail. The Green Corps have got a lot of discretion."

"Yeah, so I've heard," said Turner. "I would have thought that the Green Corps would have been pleased if someone was collecting weather data. Was it some sort of hobby for you?"

Callister laughed. "I used to work at a university in Sydney," he said. "In fact, people used to call me Professor Callister. I headed a unit called the Climate and Meteorological Study Group. We had a network of people all around the country who sent information to us, and we consolidated it into a database. For a long while, in fact, we operated under a generous government grant. Even for a couple of years after the Declaration."

"And what did the information tell you?" said Turner.

Callister laughed again. "Nothing," he said.

Turner started. "I don't get it," he said. "If you were collecting all that stuff, how could it tell you ... nothing?"

"Well, I mean ... nothing significant," said Callister. "Which is itself significant. Sure, there were hot days, hot months, hot years even, and then days and months and years that weren't. There was rain, sometimes floods, and sometimes there was no rain and then there was a drought. Then rain, and sun, and ... well, you get the picture. Cycles. Someone wrote a poem about it once."

"But I thought that it had got hotter. I've heard a lot about that. Believe me, a lot."

"You mean, the warming that was observed during the '90s?

Sure, there was an important period when the trends all pointed upwards. But when you put that together with the decades after that, and put it all into historical patterns, it didn't really mean much. We've always had hot spells, sometimes pretty long ones. The worst drought ever seen in Australia, for example, was at the end of the nineteenth century. It was called the Federation Drought. It's the way it goes. Climate changes over time, so does weather. That's what happens. Seems to be its nature.

"But the government didn't want to hear about it. They thought the whole idea of natural variability was heresy, they told us that capitalism was to blame, and it had to be. They wanted us to change the figures but we said no, the data said what it said. And then one day the Green Corps showed up and took away the computers with all the information, my unit was disbanded, and I was told that I was no longer a professor. I got this keepsake instead."

He pulled up his sleeve. There was a tattoo: DENIER.

"After all that had happened, I came to Tamworth, because my wife was from here, originally. But I kept collecting data, just in a small way, you know, some gauges in the back yard, that sort of thing. The local Green Corps didn't like it any more than the ones in Sydney, and they found out about it, I guess on one of their routine snoops on people with marks. So here I am. I'm hoping that they'll keep me here for another week or so and then let me go, tell me not to do it again. Advice I will probably ignore. My wife tells me that collecting weather stats is in my blood."

"Well, good luck with that," said Turner. He showed Callister his own mark. Callister gave an appreciative whistle.

"I'm thinking we should start a club," Turner said. "Would be pretty large. Tell me something, Professor, did you do any work on sea levels?"

"A bit, we collected some figures."

"One of the books that I heard about when I was on a prison farm said that a lot of the coastline would be flooded. You know about that?"

"Oh, that stuff from the guy that became Governor-General? And then President, after the government announced all the changes on that side of things."

"Yeah, I think that was it. There was a Green Corps guy who told me that Newcastle would go under. Did that happen?"

"No, the only rise in sea levels that anyone could find anywhere in the country was a couple of centimetres. But last I heard, Newcastle was a ghost town. Whole place was abandoned, I think. That was because the economy of the place was based on industries that simply ceased to exist, nothing to do with sea levels. I don't know where everyone who had lived there went. Somewhere else, I assume. Did you come from there?"

"All that," said Turner, "was a long time ago."

"Sometimes, it seems like everything was," said Callister. "But you didn't really answer my original question. Why are you in jail with me?"

17. McDonalds

Armidale to Tamworth was a little over a hundred kilometres, according to the McDonalds map. He had stopped at several BDSed McDonalds overnight; he had found that the back rooms were usually untouched, more or less. That made a certain sense, he thought, if the people doing the smashing had mainly seen it as a show. A performance to give an indication to others of what they could do, what they would do. Making a statement.

In one of them he had found some things in a storeroom. A pad of paper, with a yellow cardboard cover and metal spiral binding. A couple of lead pencils. A little clear plastic envelope with a box of coloured pencils and some games for kids. Cartoon figures to be coloured in, a funny little maze with a hamburger at the end. He remembered getting things like that for Ben and Livy when they had been little, years and years ago. Useful for keeping them occupied on a long drive, so they didn't start fighting in the back seat. Not really knowing why, he put the little bag into his pack.

He looked at the pad for a long time, wondering what he could do with it and turning the lead pencils over in his hands. After a while, he wrote something on the first page. A few lines about a little girl with a sore arm. Then something else. Then something more. When he stopped, he realised he had been writing for a long time, and several pages of the notebook had been filled.

"Huh," he said to himself.

18. Business

The sun was high in the sky, and burning hot, when he rode into Tamworth. In the main street, he got off the bike and pushed it along. There were some stores open, people buying or selling or trading, in the small-scale way that was the usual pattern now.

He came to a rickety plastic table, where a boy and a girl were standing under a tattered umbrella. A man and a woman were sitting a little distance away, watching the kids. There was a pitcher of something on the table and a couple of battered plastic tumblers.

"You look hot, mister," said the boy to Turner. "You look like you need a drink of juice."

"We picked the fruit and squeezed it ourselves," said the girl.

Turner looked at the handwritten sign saying how much it was.

"I think I've got enough money for that," he said to them. He took the coins out of his pocket and handed them over. The girl poured him a drink and gave it to him.

He drank. It wasn't very good. Awful, in fact. He looked at the two kids, smiling up at him.

"Mighty fine," he said. "Just what I needed."

"You want another?" said the boy.

"Uh, no, that's enough for me," said Turner.

The two adults came over. "Thanks," whispered the woman to Turner. "Their first sale."

"Might be a reason for that," said Turner to her. He thought of something. He opened his pack and took out the envelope of

McDonalds games. He handed it to the kids. "This is for you," he said to them. "Since you worked so hard at making your drink."

The kids took it and looked at it. "Wow," said the girl, softly. They stared.

"Good of you," said the kids' father. "Thank you."

"Yeah, mine used to like things like this," said Turner. "You know, I remember a time when no kid this age would be happy with anything less than a Nintendo."

The man nodded. "But these ones are too young to remember anything before the Declaration," he said.

"And just what have we here?" said a voice from behind them.

Damn, thought Turner. *Goddamn.*

He looked around. There was a Green Corps squad, six of them. The leader was looking at him, with a smile like a leather glove. "Looks like we have a stranger, making trouble," he said.

"I'm just passing through," said Turner. "I'll be moving straight on, if that's alright with you."

"Maybe, maybe, maybe," said the guy. "Don't rush."

Suddenly, Turner realised that he had his sleeves rolled up to the shoulders. *Goddamn*, he thought again.

The GC guy was looking at the table, at the jug and the glasses and the sign and the kids.

"This ... wouldn't be ... a business ... would it?" he said. "An ... unregistered ... business? Because, you know, that's illegal." He looked at the boy and the girl. And then at the parents. "You know that, right?" he said to the man and the woman. "Illegal."

"They just wanted to have a bit of fun, make a little money," said the mother. "Really, it's nothing, just a bit of fun for them."

The GC guy sighed. "Make a little money," he said. "Yes, that's always how it starts."

"They're just kids," said the father. "You can't – "

Turner saw one of the squad members take a taser from his pocket. There was a little spark of electricity. The two kids jumped.

"Can't ... what?" said the squad leader.

"Believe me," said Turner, "these kids have got no sense of business at all. Try some of their drink, if you want to see for yourself."

The GC guy stared at him. "Huh," he said. "Maybe I will." He poured some of the juice into a tumbler and sipped it. Then he spat it out. "Damned if the Recal isn't right," he said to the others in the squad.

"First time for everything," said one of them.

Then the squad leader saw the packet of games. He took it out of the girl's hands and scrutinised it. Saw the logo on the front. He touched the sticker, rubbed it slightly.

"This yours?" he said to the kids. "This ... thing?"

"No," said Turner, stepping between the squad leader and the little table. "It's mine."

"You sure?" said the GC guy.

Turner nodded.

"Because ... that would be ... bad," said the guy.

Turner said nothing.

The guy sighed again. "You see," he said to Turner, "I don't really think it's yours. I think it's theirs. Maybe I can let them off on the charge of running an unregistered business, since they're so bad at it. But having this – "

"It's mine," said Turner again.

The guy stared as Turner.

"That will cost you," he said.

Turner had heard those words before. Different type of place, same type of voice. *That will cost you …*

"You know," said Turner, "you guys really are c — "

And then the taser hit him.

19. Shot

It was the day after. He and Callister had been given some food and water by a grumpy-looking civilian, but aside from that no-one had come to the cell.

Eventually, someone – not a Green Corps member, the same person who had brought them the meal – came to the cell. She unlocked the door and gestured for Turner to come out.

"What about me?" said Callister. The woman shrugged, locked the door again, and put the keys on a hook on the other side of the room. She led Turner to an office and said he should go in.

There was a Green Corps man sitting at a desk. "Come in and shut the door," he said to Turner. "Take a seat."

Turner did, and helped himself to water from a jug on the desk.

This Green Corps guy was older than most, Turner thought. That was odd: most of them were in their twenties, had joined up as teenagers or close to it.

The man lifted something onto the desk. It was Turner's backpack.

"This is yours," said the man. It was not a question.

Turner said nothing.

"My name is Dyson," said the Green Corps man. "Like the vacuum cleaner."

Turner didn't know what that meant. It sounded like it might be a joke, but he was not in a mood to laugh.

"And your bike is outside," said Dyson. "With the rest of your stuff."

The two of them looked at each other.

Turner poured himself another glass of water.

"I sort of run things around here," said Dyson.

"If you say so," said Turner.

"I'm sorry about the taser thing," said Dyson. "Some of these young guys ... well, they think they're creating the Socialist Republic of Tamworth or something."

"Huh," said Turner. "Okay, apology accepted. Now, if you'll just give me my bag I'll be on my way."

"Not just yet," said Dyson. He started to take things out of the pack, lining them up neatly on the desk. Obviously, he had already been through it.

Finally, he took the Glock out. He put it between them.

"That's a pretty serious offence, you know," said Dyson.

"Yeah," said Turner. "I know."

"And you already have a reputation as a recalcitrant fellow," said Dyson.

"That's what the tatt says," said Turner. "Sort of."

Dyson began to put everything back into the bag. The McDonalds map, the pad and pencils, the bottle of water, the set of tools, the torch, the packets of dried meat and fruit, the other stuff. Until only the gun was left.

There was a long silence between them.

Then Dyson, softly, slowly, almost as if he was alone in the room, said: "It wasn't meant to be like this, you know. When it all started out, we thought we had an obligation to protect the environment. Protect the world. Stop the emissions, save the rivers, conserve the resources, all of that. And the people in the

Green Corps, all of us, we were all committed, committed to the cause and committed to de Silva. Damn, we knew, we just *knew* we were doing the right thing. But as it went on, other people came in. Young guys, they hardly understood what it was all about, a lot of them just liked the uniform and the fact they could … well …"

Turner remained silent, staring at Dyson.

"You used to be a cop, right?" said Dyson to him. "This is a police gun, isn't it?"

Turner nodded.

There was another silence. Turner realised that Dyson's eyes were fixed on the Glock.

Suddenly: "It wasn't meant to be this way!"

And then Turner saw, as if he was watching a scene in a movie unfold in slow motion, Dyson pick up the gun, flick the safety catch off, put the barrel to his temple, and pull the trigger. One shot.

Dyson slumped onto the desk, in a spreading pool of his own blood.

Turner jumped to his feet. He expected the door to be flung open and a Green Corps squad to come rushing in. But there was nothing.

He remembered that Dyson had told him to shut the door.

The gun was still in Dyson's hand. Turner took it and put it into the pack, into its special pocket. He wondered if he should say something over the man's body, some words that might mean something. It sounded as if he had had, after all, good intentions.

But Turner could think of nothing to say. He did not know what good intentions were worth, if they were worth anything. So he left the office, and went outside to where his bike was leaning against a wall.

Then he thought of something. He went back inside and made his way back to the cell. He took the keys from the hook and opened the door.

"Thanks," said Callister. "But what – "

"But nothing," said Turner. "I would say that Tamworth is looking at regime change in the near future. Might be good, might not be, I don't know. One way or another, I plan to get as far away as I can, as fast as I can. You might want to do the same, it's up to you."

Callister nodded. "Thank you," he said again.

"What, for letting you out of this thing?" said Turner.

"No," said Callister. "For calling me professor. Long time since anyone did that."

They shook hands.

And then Turner was running back to his bike, and was on the road, moving fast, as fast as he could pedal, didn't look back, and in a while he passed a broken sign saying that he was leaving Tamworth, thank you for visiting. After that he told himself to slow down, conserve his energy, have some water, check the map for the next McDonalds or whatever.

Going south. Again, or maybe still.

20. Toll

The bridge had seen better days but it looked like it would get him across. Nevertheless, he got off the bike and began to push it. A sign said that it was the Warego River below.

He was nearly at the other end when four men stepped out of the bushes. Two of them held sawn-off shotguns, and one was carrying something that looked like a golf club. Seven iron.

The one that seemed to be the leader stood in Turner's way. He was the biggest of them, although he wasn't carrying anything. Turner stopped a couple of metres from the little group. He imagined they would get to the point sometime. He took off his pack.

The big guy, no longer young but still carrying a good amount of muscle, put his thumbs in his belt. "This is a toll road," he said. "A fee is involved."

"For what?" said Turner.

The guy looked around. He smiled. "Bridge repairs and maintenance," he said.

"Then I guess that means you don't get too many people coming through here," said Turner.

"No, not too many," said the guy. "But enough." He named a sum. "You got that?" he said.

"Even if I did, I don't think I'd give it to you," said Turner. "But maybe I've got something else that might interest you." He reached into his pack, into the pocket at the bottom.

And then the Glock was in his hand, and pointing at the four of them.

"Meet my little friend," he said. He made a show of flicking off the safety catch.

The big guy started. The men with the shotguns shifted uneasily on their feet.

"But we've got two and you've only got one," said the leader. "You won't be able to kill us all."

"Don't have to," said Turner to him. "Here's how it might go down. I shoot you, and the other guys shoot me. Or I shoot you, and the other guys run. Or I shoot you, and the other guys cheer and break out the beer. You see a common thread here?"

The big man gave a sigh. "I have to say I do," he said. "So we have a stand-off."

"Uh-uh, don't think to," said Turner. "Those shotguns are so old I doubt they would shoot anything but cobwebs. You don't believe me, give it a try, see if you still got both hands at the end.

"But what I've got here is a Glock 7-mil, police issue. You know the best thing about Glocks? Their reliability. They come with a twenty-year guarantee."

"How do we know it's loaded?" said Seven Iron.

"Find out," said Turner, pointing it at him.

Seven Iron thought about it. "Yeah, okay," he said eventually. "Take your word for it."

"You must really want to get to Dubbo," said the big guy.

"Not particularly," said Turner. "It's on my way to somewhere else."

"Huh," said the big guy. "Where, exactly?"

"Canberra," said Turner.

"Huh," said the guy again. "And why would anyone want to go to Canberra, these days?"

"Something I have to do there," said Turner. "Thought I might introduce Mr de Silva to my travelling companion here. One way or another, I intend to get there, and you guys aren't enough to stop me."

The guy stared at him. Then he burst out laughing. So did the others.

Eventually, they stopped. "Not a bad idea, not bad at all," said the big guy. "Although I heard that the person who is really in charge is that woman Corby. Used to be a senator. Called the Director now, ever since the Declaration. That was her idea, apparently. That's what I heard."

Turner considered. He remembered the name. Remembered seeing her face on television. "I'll bear that in mind," he said.

"And just what do you have against our beloved leaders, who are doing their best to build a green tomorrow for us?" said the big guy.

"A number of things," said Turner. He pulled back his sleeve to show his mark.

The big guy gave a grunt.

"Now, are you going to let me pass?" Turner said. "Or do we have to have a more vigorous discussion? I've got enough bullets for all of you, with enough left to do what I have to do."

The big guy laughed again. Then he stepped aside, and gestured for the others to do the same. Turner, pushing his bike and with the Glock still in his hand, went through.

"I know this might not be any of my business," he said, as he got onto the bike, "but you fellas might like to think about getting into a different line of work. Not enough people travelling these days, from what I've seen. Collecting tolls might not be a viable enterprise."

The big guy gave a little nod. "We'll bear that in mind," he said.

"Hey," said Seven Iron. "About the Canberra thing. Good luck with it. We mean that."

Turner looked at the little group. "Thanks," he said. He was about to ride off when the big guy lifted his own sleeve, showed his mark. Same as Turner's.

"One Recal to another," he said.

Turner nodded. Then he set off.

21. Cold

He lay awake in the darkness. It was cold, and he was glad of the warmth of the sleeping bag. The chill made him think about what Callister had told him. After all the book readings and speeches he had sat through on the farm, all the dire warnings that he half-remembered from old television talk shows, he had assumed that there must have been something in it. But now that he thought about his own experiences, what Callister had said sounded right.

He had spent most of his early years in Newcastle, met Jean there, she had been over from New Zealand, visiting friends that lived there. Newcastle was alright, as places went, not a bad place to grow up, not a bad town to raise a couple of kids. For a long time, there had been enough work for a competent electrician, and he had all his papers.

But that work dried up pretty quickly when the blackouts started. In some ways, the brownouts were almost worse, because they were unpredictable, more frustrating than anything else. First it was for a couple of hours a day, then a few more, and then suddenly there were more hours without power than with it. Hard on the kids, teenagers by that time.

Like a lot of other people, Turner had put it down as a temporary thing, as de Silva said, in a big speech a year or so after the election. Temporary, and the cost of keeping the planet from getting hot. That was worth a bit of inconvenience, wasn't it? And soon there would be enough electricity from wind turbines and solar panels and wave generators and geothermal plants and all the other things. Free and constant. That was the story. That was the promise.

But one way or another, the power shortages meant that there was not much demand for electricians, no matter how many certificates you had. In hindsight, he should have realised where things were heading when he took a short-term job, trying to fill the gaps in the budget. It was dismantling the local coal-fired power station. Bolt by bolt, plank by plank, brick by brick. He had asked the project manager, a guy from one of the new agencies in Canberra, why they were doing it. The guy had smiled, tapped the side of his nose, and said, "just in case". Turner had had no idea what he had meant.

It was after that job that he had heard that the police were recruiting, so he had put his name down. Lot of people did. It was one of the few growth areas for employment. He had been one of the lucky ones. If you could call it that. Downside was that you had no say in where you were sent after training.

There was a theory that the government didn't like cops working in the same community they grew up in, with people they knew. Turner didn't know if that was true but when he was working in Brisbane he had asked around. Nearly everyone, certainly everyone working on the frontline, was from somewhere else. Maybe that meant something, maybe it didn't. Maybe it was just coincidence.

Growing up in Newcastle, he had never really paid much attention to the weather, despite all the warnings and predictions about climate change. As a boy, he had loved the sea, and his family had lived near it. When he had been a young man he always had better things to think about, and when he had become a man with a family there was a lot more to deal with. Now he looked back, there did not seem to have been much in the way of change. Yes, sometimes it was hot, and you took the kids to the beach, sometimes it was cold, and then you made sure they had a jumper in their school bags. Sometimes there were bushfires in the area, sometimes there were storms. As there always had been.

So maybe Callister had been right, with his data and his computers and his gauges in the backyard. No reason to think he wasn't.

He listened to the sound of the rain on the metal roof of the McDonalds. That was why they were here, an overnight stop. Because the wipers didn't work.

Even in the darkness, even with her dark skin, he could make out her profile as she slept. She gave a little murmur and moved slightly. He pulled the sleeping bag over her. So she would not be cold.

22. Lift

Funny how even a small thing can spell disaster, he said to himself, as he examined the punctured tyre. He looked down the highway one way, and then the other. Yeah, this was nowhere, alright, and he was in the middle of it. He looked up at the sun. There were already ripples of heat dancing on the asphalt, and it wasn't even noon. There were grimy clouds forming on the horizon but for the moment it was the heat that was the problem.

If he tried to ride the bike like this he would simply break the wheel, probably within five kilometres or so. He sighed and started to push. It was going to be a long haul to the next town.

He had been slogging along for over an hour when he heard a noise behind him. He looked back. It was a ute, battered but tearing along the highway in a cloud of dust and smoke.

It wheezed to a halt next to him. An indigenous woman, with battered sunglasses and her hair tied back by a red scarf, leaned out the window. "Nice day for a walk, eh?" she said. "You need a lift?"

Turner kept his eyes down. "I don't want any trouble, ma'am," he said.

The woman burst into laughter. "Ma'am!?" she said. "Ha! I haven't been called ma'am in years! And even then it was just once!"

Turner said nothing. He remembered hearing stories about how the Indigenous Compensation Act worked.

The woman stopped laughing. Then she said, more seriously: "Hey, mate, I'm offering you a lift. Or you can walk to the next town if you like. Not really something I'd recommend trying, though."

Turner looked down the empty road. "How far is it?" he said.

"About a hundred K. Or you can go back to Dubbo, which is about a hundred and twenty, I think. You might survive. Might not. If the heat doesn't get you the rain that's coming probably will."

Damn puncture, thought Turner.

"You have a vehicle," said Turner.

"Yes, Mister Obvious, I do. That's how I can offer you a lift. It might not be much but it gets the job done. Usually."

So Turner put his bike into the back – there was a heap of other stuff there, including cans of petrol – and climbed into the passenger side of the ute. They rumbled off.

After a while, the woman said: "I'm Natalie. You probably couldn't pronounce my second name, so just Natalie is fine."

Some more time passed. Natalie said: "The way this works is that you are supposed to tell me your name now."

After a few more minutes, he said: "Turner. That's it." He looked around at the rather bare interior of the ute. "I haven't been in a vehicle for a while. Last one was a bus to a prison farm. It broke. Where did you get this one?"

"Had it for a long time," said Natalie. "I come from a community a couple of hours drive away, see. Indigenous, mainly. Couple of others mixed in, various types. For leavening, my dad used to say. I'm doing a trading run to Holcroft, which is the next town along this road. Got some contacts there."

"Where do you get the petrol for it?" said Turner.

"We've got a tanker," said Natalie. "Had it for, I guess it would be about seven years or so. It must have been one of the last ones, since all the terminals were shut down around then. If I understand it right, the tanker was on its way to a depot, but when it got there the driver found the place had been hit by a BDS group. Not much left. The fella drove around for a while, wondering what to do, and eventually he ended up with us. So we bought it from him, cash. Nowhere near what it was worth, but then it wasn't really his to sell anyway, right? He went off in the mover and we didn't see him again. Since we've only got three vehicles, it's lasted us pretty well."

"Interesting story," said Turner.

"Yeah, not bad. You got one?"

Turner considered. Eventually he said: "No, not really."

"Huh," said Natalie. "Hey, you got any kids?"

Turner looked out the window at the passing landscape.

"I said, you got any kids?" said Natalie.

23. Indonesia

It was a few weeks before Paterson Square, maybe a bit longer, Turner couldn't remember exactly. It was at the little flat in Brisbane.

"We're heading north," said Ben.

"How far?" said Turner.

"Far as we can get," said Livy. "There are still a few trains running to Cape York. If we can get up there, we might be able to get a boat to PNG. From there to Indonesia, maybe. It's a bit safer than trying to get directly to Indonesia from Darwin or Broome. That's what we've heard, anyway. They're intercepting a lot of the boats, towing them back."

"The people running those boats, whether to PNG or anywhere else, are not exactly legit," said Turner. "You don't buy tickets and get a refund if it doesn't work out."

"Yeah, we know," said Ben. "We've got some cash, whatever we could save. Mum gave us as much as she could spare. She asked us to tell you that she might not be able to get here for a while, because of that. And the trains from Newcastle have gone down to one every couple of weeks now."

Turner scratched his chin. "You sure about this?" he said. "You clear on what this means?"

Livy shrugged. "Bottom line is that there's no future here for us," she said. "There was a bunch of Green Corps people at the uni a fortnight ago. Going through the enrolment records. Taking the names of everyone who had been through the Business Studies faculty, or was in it at the moment. So that means my name is on one of their lists. Just a question of time. Guess I should have studied something else."

"Hey, maybe you should have done economics," said Ben to his sister. "That's really useful. No, wait, it isn't. Because there isn't an economy to speak of anymore. That's why my Masters degree qualified me for the restaurant business."

"At least you were able to get a job, after the banks went down," said Turner. "Lot of people couldn't."

"Yeah, but waiting on tables is a dying vocation," said Ben. "Not much food to serve means no customers, which means no restaurants, which means no need for waiters. Or even people to wash dishes."

"I've heard that Australians can sometimes get jobs in one of the Indonesian resorts," said Livy. "So maybe your experience will be useful, Ben."

Turner looked at his children. He felt strangely ... *proud* ... of them. He was quiet for a long time. "I guess this is goodbye, then," he said. "I'm sorry about that, but I understand. In your position I would probably be doing the same."

A tear ran down Livy's cheek. She wiped it away with the back of her hand.

"You could come with us, Dad," said Ben. "Meet up with Mum later, maybe. Lot of tradies working in Indonesia, Malaysia, Singapore if they can get in. Some are doing well enough, apparently. You used to be an electrician, Dad, so you've got some skills that are worth something. Sparkies are in demand, with the economy there doing so well, I've heard."

"I think I might be a bit old to be starting again," he said. "And anyway, I have a job."

"Until the Green Corps decide they don't need cops anymore," said Livy. "It's not like they liked you much to start with. They'll get rid of the lot of you when they think they can."

"Not much chance of that," said Turner. "In any case, I've got a going-away present for you. Might be useful."

He led Ben and Livy into the other room and pulled up a section of loose carpet, and then a loose floorboard. In the little compartment was an envelope. He took it out and handed it to them. "One of the advantages of being a cop," he said, "is that I got some advance notice of the bank nationalisation. They cancelled everyone's leave because they needed extra people to handle the riots. I managed to get this out before things got bad. $4,200. Take it, you'll need it."

Ben stared at the envelope. "We can't do that," he said.

"It's an awful lot of money," said Livy. "You might need it yourself, Dad."

Turner took the bills from the envelope. He separated some from the stack and put those back into the envelope. He folded the rest into a roll, so it was not clear how much was there.

He handed the roll to them. "Even split," he said.

Ben looked at him. "Dad – " he said.

"Thanks," said Livy. She took it and put it into her bag. "Thanks … for everything."

He hugged each of them. "Stay together," he said. "Look after each other. That's your best bet."

They nodded, the two of them. There were plenty of stories of what had happened to people trying to make the run alone.

Then there was nothing more to say. There are times when words are not enough.

After they had gone, Turner put the envelope with the two hundred dollars into the compartment under the carpet. Then he sat down on the little couch. He sat there until it grew dark, and he sat there until it became light again.

Still staring at the horizon, he said: "No. Not now."

24. Candles

The rain came down, in sheets. The road in front of them vanished in a grey blur.

"It's only about another twenty Ks to Holcroft but I don't think we're going to make it," said Natalie. "Especially because the wipers don't work. This is a dead straight road but going on is just asking for trouble."

Turner took the map from his pack and studied it. "There's a place up ahead we can stop," he said. "Wait the rain out."

Natalie, focused on guiding the ute through the soup, nodded in agreement.

In a few minutes, a ruined McDonalds came into view. "You know, I've passed this place dozens of times but never had a reason to stop," Natalie said. "You think there'll be shelter here?"

"I've been to a few of them, and the back rooms are usually intact," said Turner.

Natalie pulled the ute into the covered laneway that had once been the drive-through. They went inside.

The front part of the building was smashed, water streaming in through the ceiling, but there was a dry storeroom at the back. They found a couple of chairs.

"Is this how you've been moving around?" said Natalie. "Going from one McDonalds to another?"

"Useful things," said Turner. "But there's been enough little towns and other places to stop as well. I've managed to get a bit of work, fixing electrical things mainly. Made enough cash to keep eating, or got paid in food."

"Where're you heading?"

"South."

"For work?"

He looked at her. "Not exactly," he said eventually.

"Meaning you don't want to tell me," she said. "In case it doesn't work out?"

"No," said Turner. "In case it does."

The rain continued, and it began to grow dark. Natalie went to the ute and returned with a couple of candles, which she lit. Turner took some food from his pack and they shared it.

"You know," said Natalie, "I used to really like McDonalds. Especially the fries."

"Yeah, me too," said Turner. "What do you have at the place you come from? Is it a farm?"

"We grow a fair bit of stuff, and collect some as well. There's plenty of kangaroos about too," she said. "Easy hunting."

"You hunt with spears?" said Turner.

"Uh, why would we do that?" said Natalie.

"Well, I thought that's what indigenous communities did," said Turner. "That's what they told us at the farm where I used to … er, live."

"Yeah, you mentioned that you'd been on one," said Natalie.

Turner gave a little shrug, not knowing what to say. "Wasn't too bad a place, really," he said. "Enough to eat, but it was all pretty boring. Could have done without the lectures, though."

Natalie laughed. "Well, if it was the Green Corps that told you that we hunted with spears, you can add it to the list of things they don't know. Long list. No, no spears. We have rifles. Someone thought it would be a good idea to buy a couple of thousand bullets, when things started to slip."

"Someone?" said Turner.

She laughed again. "Okay, it was me," she said.

Turner said nothing.

They continued to listen to the rain.

After a while, Turner said: "Is this where you've always lived? Around here? At your community?"

"Hell no," said Natalie. "I grew up there but I lived in the big smoke for a while, came back when the power started to fail. That's how I got the bullets, from some army guy who was selling them to get enough cash for a ticket out. I was – you'll laugh at this – a hairdresser. Pretty good one. Hey, you look like you could use a trim."

Turner looked at her, silent.

"You remind me of my brother," said Natalie. "He doesn't smile either. Tell me something, when I stopped for you today, why didn't you want to get in?"

He shrugged. "I was thinking about the Indigenous Compensation Act," he said. "The law the government brought in a couple of months after the Declaration. Didn't it say that indigenous people could claim any piece of property they wanted? Anything from a farm to a, well, a bicycle."

"Ha!" said Natalie. "That thing! If the damn government had actually asked us we would have told them it was a really stupid thing to do. No-one I ever heard of used it like that, or even at all. But there were plenty of lawyers who made a pretty good living out of making claims. On behalf of indigenous people, they said, although I never saw any benefit going to them. But the lawyers must have made enough money to move overseas, because I haven't seen any of them around for years."

Turner considered. Then he said: " 'The first thing we do, let's kill all the lawyers'."

"*Henry VI*," said Natalie. "Shakespeare. I remember doing it in school."

"Me too," said Turner. "Fair while ago, though."

In the candlelight, they looked at each other. The rain continued to drum on the roof.

"Looks like we're here for the night," said Natalie. "I've got a sleeping bag in the back of the ute. You got one?"

Turner nodded.

Natalie looked around the little storeroom. "Enough room here for two," she said. "You over there, me here. You okay with that?"

"Yes," said Turner. "I'm okay with that."

25. Trade

They pulled into the little town of Holcroft, to a shop that had once doubled as a petrol station. There was a trio of windmills in a field not far away. Cows and sheep grazed amongst them.

Turner helped Natalie take a number of packages from the back of the ute and carry them in. There was an older, solidly-built guy behind the counter, and an equally solidly-built woman on a stool next to him. She was knitting.

"G'day, Nat," said the guy. "Who's your friend?"

"G'day," said Natalie. "He's Turner. Turner, this is Tank."

Turner shook hands with the guy. "Why Tank?" he said.

Tank showed him the tattoo on his arm. SCEPTIC. No, thought Turner, as he re-read it. It said SEPTIC.

"Huh," he said.

"Fellow got it wrong," he said. "Probably. So now everyone calls me Tank."

"Not everyone, darl," said the woman.

"Well, everyone but Bev here," said Tank.

"Least they spelled mine right," said Bev, showing Turner her own.

Turner lifted his sleeve. "Guess they considered 'recalcitrant' a bit too much work," he said.

Natalie unwrapped one of the packages. It was several dozen beeswax candles.

"Great," said Tank. "No trouble moving them. Turner, these

things are like gold. Candles and paper, that's what's really valuable these days. Nat, we've got some beef, if you want to take it back with you."

"Fine, we're a bit sick of kanga bangers," said Natalie.

"Beef?" said Turner. "Is that allowed? I thought the Green Corps didn't like that. The Animal Protection Act, I think."

"Don't worry, this one died of natural causes," said Bev. "Heart attack. Brought on by a life of indulgence and over-eating. That's our story."

"Funny how often it happens," said Tank. "Although I suppose we could always tell the Green Corps that we are doing our bit to cut down greenhouse gas emissions. Cows are notorious for that."

"Flatulence," said Bev, still knitting.

"Huh," said Turner again.

"Turner here can do electrical work," said Natalie. "Maybe he can do something about your turbines. They go around, Turner, but there's no power."

"I'll give it a try," said Turner.

It was several hours later. Turner was working on the junction box when Natalie came up to him.

"Making progress?" she said.

"Water had got into the system, shorted out the switches," said Turner. "Not too hard to fix, if you know how."

"Tank and Bev will insist on giving you something for this, you know."

"Well, I'm not going to tell them they can't. Is that how you do everything around here, through barter?"

"Pretty well. For a while, we were passing cash back and forth.

Then we realised that we were just using the same notes, over and over. Not like the government was printing any new ones, right? No paper being made, no plastic, not even any metals for coins being mined, and no-one trusted the government bank. So Tank and I gave the money thing up and started doing stuff-for-stuff trade. Tank will trade the candles and the other things from my community for whatever he can get from whoever he can get it from, and give it to me next visit. He has a good idea of what my lot need.

"And there can be a problem with cash. He told me once that a Green Corps squad turned up one day and said he had too much money. That was after they got the tatts. Money made him a class exploiter, they said. So they cleaned out his cash register, said it was a fine. You want to know the funny part? Tank used to be the secretary of the local Labor Party branch. So he and Bev got a good laugh out of the class exploiter thing."

"What, they just … took it?" said Turner.

"Not the first time I've heard of it," she said. "They started doing things like that after the police force was disbanded. After that, the Green Corps could do pretty much whatever they wanted. They might not have guns but they have vehicles – God knows where their petrol comes from – and those sticks they carry. Some have tasers. That might not sound like much, maybe, but it's enough when everyone else has got nothing."

Turner was listening while he worked. He admitted to himself that he liked listening to Natalie talk. But he did not know how to tell her that. So he said nothing.

He spliced the final wires together and screwed the box shut. They went into the store. Natalie flipped the wall switch, and the light came on. There was the creaking rumble of a refrigerator starting up.

"Now this," said Tank, "calls for a celebration."

"Yes, it does," said Bev. "Not that you need an excuse, darl. The new batch ready?"

"Sure is," said Tank. "We can even make it cold now."

"Now that's good news," said Natalie.

"New batch of what?" said Turner.

26. Infiltration

Holcroft's idea of a celebration, as it turned out, was an evening bonfire in the little town square, a trio of rambunctious musicians, and plates of food being passed around.

Turner was sitting on a bench, wondering if it had been a good idea to allow Natalie to cut his hair. In return for the turbines, she had said, and she would not be put off by his reluctance. Determined woman.

Tank and Bev came up to him. "Thanks for the repairs," said Tank. "But somehow I don't think you're just drifting around the country with a set of screwdrivers."

"We saw you, we thought that there's a man with some serious mischief on his mind," said Bev. "Is that the case?"

Turner looked at them, wondering how much he should say. "Might be," he said eventually.

"Huh," said Tank. "Where you heading, Turner?"

Turner was silent for a few moments, and then said: "Canberra. I'd appreciate it if you didn't tell Natalie that. There might be ... consequences. Questions asked."

"Okay, if you that's what you want," said Tank.

"Maybe you can fill in some blanks for me," said Turner. "Natalie said you used be something in the Labor Party, Tank. What was the story there? I never knew what happened, in the years before the Declaration. Guess I wasn't really paying attention."

Tank laughed. "Yeah, a lot of us weren't paying attention," he said. "I was the secretary of the local branch and the co-ordinator of the regional conference. There was a series of party conferences held all over the country on the same day, a few months before the election. I was checking the credentials of members when all these young people starting coming into the hall. Blow me down if they didn't have party tickets, paid up and everything. There were dozens of them, they arrived in buses, there must have been a couple of hundred by the end. They didn't look like Labor people so I checked and double-checked. But they had the right papers, they were on the roll. So I had to let them in. Give them voting cards. That's what the rules said."

"Trots," said Bev.

"Uh, what?" said Turner.

"She means Trotskyites," said Turner. "Infiltrators. So many of them, they had a majority on the conference floor. I called head office and they told me the same thing was happening all over the place. Co-ordinated.

"Anyway, they voted out a lot of the parliamentarians, the old guard. That wasn't too bad, most of those guys had been around forever and not done anything. And then they voted for an amalgamation of Labor and the Greens, with de Silva as the leader. That bit actually made sense, because de Silva was much more popular than the Labor guy, and more popular than the conservative PM as well. Damn, we really wanted to get that bastard out, so a lot of our people thought, well, if this is what it takes to do that, we can live with it. And that's what happened, de Silva won the election. Him, and that Corby woman as deputy. And the election was, what, two years before the Declaration."

"Pity you didn't think it through, darl," said Bev.

Tank shrugged his shoulders, with the look of a man who

appreciated a good scam when he saw one, even if it had cost him. "Yeah, a real shame," he said. "Although I don't know what we could have done about it. Everything was within the rules, nice and legal. Long time in the planning, I would think."

There was a commotion on the other side of the square. It was Natalie. She was carrying a crate of mis-matched plastic bottles full of brownish liquid.

"Is that ... what I think it is?" said Turner.

"Sure is," said Tank. "Beer. Home brewed, we've got a shed in the back and we grow our own hops and barley. Cold, thanks to you fixing the windmills and giving us power for the fridge."

Natalie came over to them. She had a shiny white ribbon in her hair, and lipstick. Turner wondered when he had last seen lipstick.

She had a bottle of beer in each hand. She handed one to Turner.

"Even after everything that's happened, we're still Aussies and we still like a beer," she said, as they drank.

"Guess so," said Turner.

Natalie was watching the band, and the people dancing. She gave a little cough.

Eventually, she said: "So."

Turner sipped his beer.

Natalie sighed. "Where are you heading next?" she said to him.

"Towards Orange, I suppose," he said.

"Oh, that's on my way back," said Natalie. "I can give you a lift. I've got enough extra petrol."

"Orange?" said Bev. "Nat, that's not on your way, it's miles – "

"It's ... on ... my ... way," said Natalie, through gritted teeth.

"Oh, right," said Bev.

Natalie shifted her glare to Turner.

Tank gave a grunt. "Alright, Nat, I'll dance with you," he said. The two of them went onto the makeshift dance floor.

"You don't dance?" said Turner to Bev.

"Hip," said Bev. "What's your excuse?"

"Eight years on a prison farm," he said. "Dries you up, burns you out."

They watched Natalie and Tank and the other people of the little town doing something that might be called dancing.

"Her bloke shot through a couple of years back," said Bev. "She has some kids, teenagers or a bit more, I think. She didn't seem upset to see the fella go."

"Huh," said Turner.

"She likes you, you know," said Bev.

"Really?" said Turner. "It's been so long since I talked with a woman that I don't know how to read the signs. Not that I was ever very good at that sort of thing."

"Well, Orange isn't really on her way."

"Yeah," said Turner. "But Canberra is where I'm going. Come too far to quit now. Got to see it through, I think."

"Then you'll need this," said Bev. "Look at it as payment for the fix-it job." She pulled something from her pocket and handed it to him.

It was a bicycle tyre repair kit.

27. Effect

The voice boomed through the loudspeaker: "This is your only warning! Go back to your homes!"

Someone in the little crowd shouted back, in a cracked and hollow voice: "We don't have homes! You took them away from us!"

The Green Corps guy with the loudspeaker, the squad leader, put it down. "Okay, have it your way then," he said softly. "If you want to play it like that." He gestured to one of his people to start distribution to the line of cops.

"I don't like the look of this," said the cop next to Turner, softly, as he took one from the GC woman. "Don't like where this is going. I didn't sign up for this."

"We follow orders," said Corrigan, the leader of the police squad. "That's what we do. We're cops."

Turner looked down at what he was now holding in his hands.

"Prepare for a warning volley!" called Corrigan to his men. "Over their heads!"

"None of that bullshit!" shouted the Green Corps commander. "Aim and fire for effect!"

One of the Green Corps members pulled the tarpaulin away from what was mounted on the back of the truck. The guy got behind it, and the barrel began to swing around.

Turner couldn't move. Couldn't lift the shotgun. Couldn't –

"Wake up," said a voice.

Natalie. She was shaking him, not too gently.

"Quite a dream you were having," she said, as he sat up.

"You might say that," said Turner. He wiped his eyes. He looked around at the deserted cottage where they were spending the night. There was a candle burning. "Sorry, didn't mean to wake you," he said.

"That's alright, I wasn't asleep anyway," she said. He saw that she was wearing a pair of glasses, old-style ones with heavy black frames. They were oddly fetching. "Reading," she said. She held up Turner's pad. "Found this in your pack. Hope you don't mind."

"No," said Turner. "I don't mind."

"Interesting stuff. You've certainly covered the Ks."

"Further to go yet."

"Do you know how your story is going to end?"

"Does anyone?"

"I guess not."

There was a long silence between them.

Then Natalie said: "Turner … "

He cast a long look at her. But he said nothing.

She took off her glasses, folded them. She gave a little sigh, a gesture of recognition that sometimes the stars refused to align. "We'd both better get to sleep," she said. "Got some driving to do tomorrow."

She blew out the candle.

28. Intersection

They were standing at a junction on the northern outskirts of Orange. One of the roads led north-west.

"I have to be heading that way now," said Natalie. "Home. I don't have enough petrol to take you any further and still make it back."

"I appreciate everything you've done," said Turner.

"You ... could come with me," she said softly. "You could ... choose ... that."

He looked down the road heading through Orange. "Choosing doesn't enter into it any more," he said. "I have to do this."

She gave a rueful little smile. "Yeah, I get it," she said. "And what then?"

Turner considered. "Haven't thought that far ahead," he said.

"Think you might be heading back this way sometime?"

He scratched his stubble. "I hope so," he said.

They stared at each other.

Eventually, Turner said: "I don't know where you live."

Natalie smiled again, less rueful this time. "You can ask Tank and Bev," she said. "They know."

"Natalie," said Turner. "I don't know what's going to happen. I can't make any promises. About anything."

"I understand that," she said.

She kissed him on the cheek.

She got into the ute and started it up.

Turner watched the vehicle until it vanished over the skyline.

He took out his map and looked at it.

The cartoon face stared at him.

"Shut up, Ronald," muttered Turner.

He got onto his bike and turned south.

29. AC

Turner was cycling past a field of red flowers. There were acres of them, and further away a field of low, shrubby plants. He wondered what those were – they looked vaguely familiar – but they were too far away for him to get a good look.

He shifted on the bicycle seat, trying to get comfortable.

"Blisters on my blisters," he muttered to himself.

He was coming up to the outskirts of a town. He approached a sign: St John's Regional Hospital. There was an arrow, and he followed it, pulling off the freeway.

In a few minutes, he came to a brick building. It was one of a complex of buildings but it seemed to be the only one still functioning. There were some horses tied up in shade of some trees, and one out of three windmills on the roof of the building appeared to be working.

He dismounted – gratefully. He went inside. There were some people sitting on chairs, obviously waiting.

A middle-aged woman came up to him. "Haven't seen you before," she said. "What can I do for you, stranger?"

"Wouldn't mind seeing a doctor or someone," said Turner. "But maybe I can do something for you. I saw that two of your turbines are down. Might be able to fix them. Got my own tools. Is there a manager or someone I could talk to about it?"

"That would be me," said the woman. "I don't suppose you know how to fix an ultrasound machine?"

"No, sorry."

"MRI?"

"Don't even know what that is."

"How about an air-conditioner?"

"Depends on why it's broke. Give it a try."

The woman took off her glasses and cleaned them on the hem of her skirt. "Good enough," she said. "I'm Horsham, by the way."

"Is that Doctor Horsham?"

"No, I just try and run the place. We still have a couple of doctors and a few other medicos. Everyone does what they can, and people pay however they are able. Come with me."

She led Turner through a series of corridors. Eventually, they came to a room where a woman, maybe sixty, was lying in a bed. There was a younger man sitting next to her, reading a book aloud. Despite the open window the room was hot, stuffy, stale.

"How is my favourite patient today?" said Horsham to the woman.

"Better, I think," said the woman.

Turner didn't think she looked better.

"Good to hear," said Horsham. She pointed to an air-conditioner on the wall.

"Let's take a look," said Turner. He took his tools from his pack and began to dismantle the unit. Eventually, he said to Horsham: "This is going to take a while, I'll have to take the whole thing apart and re-wire it. If you've got other things you have to do, go ahead."

Horsham nodded. She turned to the woman in the bed. "April, just because I'm leaving doesn't mean you can make a pass at our friend here," she said.

"Damn, you never let me have any fun," said April. She tried to laugh but it turned into a rasping choke. The younger man held a plastic container up to her and she coughed a few mouthfuls of dark blood into it.

Turner worked for about an hour. He looked around the building and found a disused room with a broken air-conditioner; it was beyond repair but still yielded some useful parts. He was replacing the housing on the one in April's room when Horsham re-appeared.

"Try it now," he said to her.

Horsham flipped the switch. There was a creaking rumble from the unit, a blast of dust, and then a stream of cool air.

"Oh, that's nice," said April.

The man shook Turner's hand. "Thank you," he said. "Thank you." There were tears in his eyes.

Turner didn't know what to say. He managed to mumble: "No worries."

Horsham led him out. Turner noticed that most of the lights of the hospital were either switched off or were not working.

"I suppose you know that if you've got only a limited amount of electricity," he said, "air-conditioning is not a very efficient way to use it."

"You want to go back and turn the one in April's room off?" she said.

"Not what I meant."

"In any case, she won't be needing it for long."

"So she'll be going home soon, will she?"

"Er, no."

It took a few moments for Turner to realise what she meant. Then he understood. "Nothing you can do?" he said.

Horsham shook her head. "You know the worst part?" she said. "When I first came to this hospital – I guess that was nearly twenty years ago – it would have been pretty easy. Radiotherapy would have taken care of it. Six doses, eight to be sure. But after the Lucas Heights reactor in Sydney was shut down there were no isotopes available. That was five days after the Declaration, if I remember it right."

Turner nodded. He thought about his grandfather, who had had radiotherapy to treat a tumour in his chest when Turner was about twelve. Guy had gone on to live to the age of 96. Died with a beer in his hand.

"At least we've got painkillers," said Horsham. "We have to make them ourselves. Even grow them ourselves."

"Huh?" said Turner. Then it clicked. "Oh, the poppies," he said.

"You saw our crop, did you? Yeah, we collect the opiate and turn it into useable drugs. Morphine, mainly. We make enough to send some to other clinics in the area, barter it for whatever might be available from them if we can. We have a guy who knows how to make it. He works in the basement. I think he used to be in the drug-making business for … well, not for legal purposes. I get the impression that he does this for us to make up for past misdemeanours. Basically, I haven't asked him too many questions."

"Useful skill, I guess," said Turner.

Horsham gave a little laugh. It sounded like something she didn't do very often. "As long as he can deliver some relief to people like April, it's fine by me," she said. "And if she wants us to help her pass, then the morphine can do that, make it easier. She wouldn't be the first one to want to go that way. Can't say that I like it, in principle, but it's preferable to the other options."

Turner thought about his blisters. Suddenly, they didn't seem like much of a problem.

"We have something else for less serious cases," said Horsham. "Marijuana. For medical purposes, of course. For people in pain, it's better than nothing. Which is the alternative. You probably saw our little plantation, near the poppies."

Turner nodded, thinking of the low shrubs. "Is that legal?" he said.

"Search me," said Horsham. "Tell the truth, it's pretty hard to know what's legal and what isn't these days. One Green Corps guy will tell you something, another one will tell you something else. I know that when we first started doing it a Green Corps squad said it was alright. As long as we gave them a packet. Which we did. Aside from opiates and dope, we've got some herbal remedies, natural stuff, things like that. Better than nothing."

"Guess so," said Turner. "Anyway, about those turbines. Maybe I can do something about those two that aren't working. If it's just a wiring problem or something like that, I might be able to get them up and running. I'll take a look at the other one as well, do whatever maintenance I can, might make it last a bit longer."

"That would be great," said Horsham. "Sorry we can't pay you for it. Unless you might take … ?"

"Don't think so," said Turner. "Used to be a cop, you see. Old habits die hard."

It was the next day. Turner had got the other turbines operating.

In return, Horsham had given him a package of fruit and vegetables from the hospital garden. And a little jar of herbal ointment as well, for which Turner was thankful.

As he was about to leave, Turner thought of April. He found his way back to her room. But it was empty.

30. Go

"Sorry it had to work out this way," said Corrigan.

Turner grimaced. He knew that none of it had been Corrigan's fault. Cops took orders from Green Corps officers, that was all there was to it. The police captain was taking a risk right now, having brought Turner back to the little flat so he could grab some possessions. If it had been up to the Green Corps commander Turner would have gone straight to jail, and then to wherever they were going to send him, no questions asked and none answered. The only stop on the way would have been the tattooist, for the mark showing that Turner had a problem with authority.

"Can you do something for me?" said Turner. "Can you get a letter to Jean?"

Corrigan's face softened. "Yeah, I think so, I'll do what I can," he said. He went out onto the little porch to give Turner a few moments of privacy to scribble a couple of lines. When that was done, Turner went into the other room, and put his service pistol into the compartment under the loose floorboards, with the envelope of cash. He didn't really know why, but he was damned if he was going to let the Green Corps get their hands on it. Six in the clip.

He changed clothes, police uniform for the civvies that looked the most likely to last. He threw some more clothes, some food, some bottles of water, into a bag.

Corrigan came in. Turner handed him the letter, and his badge.

Corrigan looked at them. "Nothing else?" he said.

"Nothing else," said Turner.

Corrigan gave a little grunt. "Okay," he said.

Turner looked around. There wasn't really anything he could see that was important to him. He hefted his bag over his shoulder.

"Let's go," he said.

31. Stand

Turner was sitting on the top of a wind turbine. This was one of the big ones, probably a one-point-five, he thought, so he was a long way up. Once, it had fed into the national grid, but those days were past. There wasn't a grid to speak of, although he had heard there were still fragments of it operating in some parts of the country.

He looked around. Spreading out from his location were rolling grasslands, low hills, a network of creeks feeding into a river which was itself shadowed by the highway. Green, yellow, occasional splashes of ochre red, all underneath an upturned bowl of clear blue. It was pastoral country, or it had been once, and there were still crops that could be seen, although they had burst out of their fences and were growing wild now. The town of Goulburn was not far over the horizon, looking south.

Closer, less than half a kilometre from the turbine, was the little community, a collection of caravans and trailers clustered around a few buildings, where he had stopped. There was a series of enclosures, one for cows, one for sheep, one for horses. The people had asked him if he could repair the turbine, perhaps rig a line to their generator. He had said he would try.

But at the moment he was simply admiring the view. It wasn't especially grand, not in the way that mountain peaks and canyons are grand, yet it had its own remarkable qualities. You had to have the right sort of eyes to see them but once you started looking they were hard to miss.

This is a damn beautiful country, he said to himself. *Not always easy to understand, not always easy on those who live in it, but damn beautiful nevertheless. Didn't deserve what has happened to it.*

"Stop daydreaming and get to work," he said aloud, to himself. He knew that he wasn't here to admire the view but to do a job. He checked that the safety belt he had rigged up was properly fastened and started to remove the turbine housing. The blades were not turning, and it did not take him long to find out why. He had never worked on a windmill this size before but he understood the principles, and he understood that there was nothing he could do. After a while, he replaced the housing and climbed down the metal ladder welded to the side of the shaft.

Mitchell was waiting for him at the bottom.

"Any luck?" she said.

"Sorry, nothing I can do," he said. "The cogs are split, both the primaries and the secondaries, and the belts are completely useless. Without parts, there's just no way to get it working."

Mitchell, apparently not surprised, nodded. They began to walk back towards the caravans and buildings. "I've heard things like it before," she said. "That was always a weak point of the renewable energy argument, wasn't it? That they need maintenance and repairs, both the machines themselves and the system they connect to. So do traditional power sources, of course, but all the radical environmentalists seemed to think that you just built these things and switched them on and they would run forever."

"Yeah, all machines will break eventually, if they're not tended to," said Turner. "It's in their nature. Of the ones I've seen, maybe only a quarter are still working. Tell the truth, I hadn't known so many had been built, both wind and solar."

"The previous government had actually done a reasonable job

at increasing the amount of renewable sources," said Mitchell. "After the election, the new government put a lot more money into it – except hydro, of course. By the time coal was outlawed and the mines were closed, very soon after the Declaration, renewables accounted for about thirty per cent of the total capacity, perhaps more. That was enough to get by for a while, with blackouts and rationing, and since there wasn't much left in the way of industry. But that didn't last.

"I remember, when the government was stopping imports and exports, thinking that getting parts was going to be a problem. I guess they thought that components could be made here, but the factories that were left couldn't get the raw materials they needed. After the takeover of the banks, no-one would invest any money, or had it to invest. So the power system gradually deteriorated. If I had to guess, I would say that the total electricity generation capacity of Australia is now no more than one gigawatt, probably less than that. Used to be about fifty-five."

Turner looked at her, not understanding the terms.

She gave a laugh which said that her life had not worked out as she had once expected. "Before all this, I ran an energy consulting firm," she said. "Sydney. We helped companies use energy more efficiently. So I knew a bit about it. Not that it helped any, in the end."

They entered the building that had once been a roadside café but now served as a communal kitchen for Mitchell's group. They sat down at one of the wooden benches. There were about a dozen other people there, most of them preparing food or repairing clothes.

"I recall de Silva saying that the government had a lot of plans for building wind turbines and solar plants themselves, rather than subsidise private companies," said Turner. "What happened to that idea?"

Mitchell shrugged, as if she had thought about the subject too much to worry about it anymore. "Didn't work out," she said. "Like a lot of things. Aside from the lack of materials, the real problem was the lack of qualified people. Everyone with the skills had either gone or were headed for the door, legally or not. You can't really blame them. But it turned out to be an awful lot of people that left the country. Asia, Europe, North America, anywhere. So many went to New Zealand that the government closed its borders to Australians. I guess they figured that two million or so was enough."

"Yeah," said Turner. "I remember that."

"One way or another," said Mitchell, "it meant that everything gradually fell apart. Power, transport, communications. Guess we got used to it, a bit at a time."

"I'm starting to think," said Turner, "that getting used to things a bit at a time is more part of the problem than part of the solution."

"Yes, you could be right about that," said Mitchell. "It's like boiling a frog."

Turner had no idea what that meant but he said nothing.

An elderly woman with a flour-stained apron around her waist and the expression of someone who loved their work came up to them and put a loaf of bread, a little tub of jam, and a pitcher of juice down. "Uh, I don't have much in the way of money," said Turner.

Mitchell laughed. "That's alright, we know you gave the turbine a shot," she said. "And we're grateful, so this is on the house. This is my mum, by the way. She's the cook here."

Turner thanked the woman for the food and drink, and she bustled away, saying she would bring some pie.

Mitchell watched her go. "You know, she's the reason I stayed here. I could have left, got a job overseas. I had the skills and some contacts, but I stayed," she said. "I thought they would need me to look after them. Mum and Dad. He died last year. As it turned out, they ended up looking after me. And the rest of us, as well, as people started showing up here and decided to stay."

She pointed to a long row of jars on a shelf. Preserved fruits, pickled vegetables, smoked meat, lots of things. Enough to last through a bad season, probably.

"I didn't realise how much she knew," said Mitchell. "How to grow things, how to store things, how to repair things. She even knew how to convert the stove to use scrap wood. Better than my degrees in science and IT, when things went down to the wire. And as for Dad, well, I'd always thought of him as the guy who put his feet up to watch the cricket on television, but he knew how to build things and keep them going. He made a bore well for us, that's really important because this area has always been prone to water shortages. He built three wagons, various sizes, and showed us how to use horses. Even ride them. He told me once he had done all that when he was young, just a teenager, but he remembered how. Remarkable, eh? When I was in business, we would have called them critical human assets."

"I guess you don't know how valuable something is until you really need it," Turner said.

Mrs Mitchell came back, with a pie, still warm. "Here you go, dearies," she said, setting it down.

At that moment, there was a sound of an engine outside. Everyone in the room froze.

The door opened and two Green Corps men came in. They looked around. They had their hands on their batons.

"What do you want?" said Mitchell to them, warily.

"We saw smoke coming from here," said one of them. "Emissions. That's a problem for you."

"I'm baking," said Mrs Mitchell. "If you don't like it, you can fuck off."

"Careful, grandma," said one of the men. "You're not too old to get a mark."

"Ha!" said Mrs Mitchell. She took off her cardigan; she was wearing a sleeveless shirt underneath. Tattoos, curling leaves and Celtic patterns, snaked down her arms, from her shoulders to her wrists. They had been there for a long time. "Think you can find a spot?" she said.

The other GC guy looked at Mitchell, sitting at the table. He saw the resemblance between the two women.

"Maybe not on you," he said to Mrs Mitchell, pointing at her daughter. "But maybe on her. We'll be able to think of some good reason, I'm sure. There's always a reason for process identification."

Suddenly, Mrs Mitchell scooped up the pie from the table and hit him in the face with it.

The other GC guy burst into laughter, pointing at his colleague.

"And as for you – " said Mrs Mitchell to him. She picked up a broom and began hitting him with it.

"Hey, stop that!" said the guy, trying to fend it off.

But she continued to whack him and poke him, and the other guy as well. The two of them started for the door. Mrs Mitchell pursued them back to their car, hitting them all the way. Mitchell and Turner and the others followed.

"We'll be back, with more people," said the guy who still had pastry clinging to his face.

"Do that," said Turner. "And make sure you tell them that you need reinforcements because you got beat by an old lady with a broom and a pie."

The two of them looked at each other. Then they got into their car and drove away.

"Heh," said Mitchell. "My mum. They don't make 'em like that anymore."

"Pricks," said Mrs Mitchell. "I've always said that you can't let the bastards grind you down. Sometimes you have to make a stand. Sometimes you have to fight. However you can, with whatever you can reach."

Turner watched the car disappear into the distance. He doubted they would be around again. "Yes," he said. "Sometimes you do."

32. Night

In a ruined McDonalds, Turner sat at a plastic table, writing by the light of the torch. The pad was almost full.

Part of him wanted to get back on the road, be moving again. But another part told him that he should rest, eat. Two hundred, two-fifty kilometres still to go, maybe more.

He put down the pencil and rubbed his eyes. He wondered where Jean was, right at this moment. He wondered if Ben and Livy had made it, had been able to build some sort of lives for themselves. He hoped so. It was painful, not knowing.

He stared through the broken windows, trying to see what was out there. Looking into the darkness, staring into the night. On the table before him were the contents of his pack. Some pieces of paper, some tools, some supplies, the gun. He wondered what they added up to.

There was another poster of de Silva on the wall. This one was different to the other one. It was more recent, and this de Silva looked stern rather than visionary, even a little angry. It was the picture of a man who was certain of his convictions, sure of his faith. A man without doubts, a man who would do Whatever It Takes. The words across the bottom were FOR FUTURE GENERATIONS.

Turner looked at it for a long time, considering where roads led.

Then he picked up the pencil and continued writing.

33. Section 47A(ii)

The sky had become a pool of dark clouds, and the first drops of rain had already begun to fall.

Up ahead, Turner could see something, a hundred metres or so from the side of the road. As he came closer, he saw that it was a shipping container, a large metal box. He had seen others in various places, presumably dumped wherever they landed when the trucks carrying them ran out of petrol, or the drivers concluded there wasn't a point anymore.

But this one looked a bit different. For one thing, there was a man standing outside it, looking up at the threatening sky. Even as Turner watched, the man saw him and waved. He was gesturing for Turner to come in. An offer of cover. Even though he wanted to continue, Turner knew that he would not get far on a soaked, slippery road. So he swung off the highway as the rain started to come down, cold and heavy. He made it before being drenched.

He dismounted, and put the bike inside the container door. The man handed him a threadbare towel.

"Thanks," said Turner. He looked around at the interior of the container. A narrow bunk, some shelves, some cupboards, an oil lantern suspended from the ceiling on a piece of string. "You live here?" he said.

"If you can call it that," said the man. "Keeps the rain out, at least. You're welcome to stay until it passes." He gestured to two chairs. They sat, and Turner introduced himself. The man said that his name was Forsythe. From his pack, Turner took some apples that he had collected from an overgrown orchard he had passed through, and they shared them.

Turner noticed that one of the shelves of the makeshift room was laden with sheaves of paper, in cardboard folders.

"Do you use that for fuel, for starting fires?" he said.

Forsythe gave a little laugh. "No, but I guess I may as well," he said. "My friend, what you are looking at there is a piece of history. You've heard of the Declaration, I take it? Well, that's how it came about."

"Huh," said Turner. "That's it, eh? How do you know?"

"Because," said Forsythe, "I wrote it. Drafted it. What parliamentary lawyers call the enabling instrument, anyway. It was my job, writing legislation that would then go into Parliament, and would be voted on. On instructions from the government, of course."

Turner took another bite of his apple. "Wouldn't mind hearing the story," he said. "I remember seeing stuff about the Declaration, when it happened, on television, but I've never heard about what led up to it."

"Really?" said Forsythe. "Most people don't want to know, just want to forget about it."

Turner looked at him.

Forsythe sighed. "I used to be a public servant," he said. "Canberra. Had a big office in a big building, not far from Parliament House. I'd worked for several governments, turning their ideas into laws and regulations, I had a good team of people. When the new government came in, I didn't think it would be much different. Sure, they brought in a whole heap of new laws, and some of them were controversial, but whether they were good or bad wasn't really my concern. And they had control of both chambers, the House and the Senate, between their own people and the various independent ones who leaned their way. In some ways that made my life a lot easier, because the previous government, the conservative one, had had to negotiate everything. Not a very efficient process, when your job is about seeing legislation passed."

"Yes, I remember that," said Turner.

"But the new government didn't have to do that, not for the first year, at least. Then some of its people, mostly ones from the old Labor Party, started to ask questions. They started to say that the sort of things the government was doing, some of the things they said they wanted to do, weren't acceptable to them. The government, especially Senator Corby, as she was then, began to think they might switch sides, bring the government down and force another election. And all the opinion polls said the government would lose, and lose badly.

"But they kept putting legislation through. The Parliament would sit until three or four in the morning, sometimes. I had to be there, in case my advice was needed. There was a special place for public servants to sit, and I'd be there, and I'd watch the parliamentarians, and half of them would be asleep at their desks. Can't really blame them, given the hours."

He took a folder from one of the shelves and showed the first page to Turner. It said METEOROLOGICAL RESEARCH FUNDING BILL.

"It was on one of those late nights, or early mornings, that Corby called me into her office," said Forsythe. "She said that she wanted to make a change to this particular bill, and she wanted me to find the right form of words for an amendment."

"Meteorological research funding?" said Turner. "You mean, studying the weather?"

"Sounds pretty innocuous, doesn't it?" said Forsythe. "What she wanted was to insert a new paragraph. Section 47A(ii), as it became." He sorted through the papers until he came to a particular part.

"She told me what she wanted, explained it all very carefully. This is what I came up with."

He read: "The government shall be enabled, by way of making a Declaration, to establish an Emergency Council to address the climate crisis, and to determine the membership of the Emergency Council. The Emergency Council shall have the power, on its own authority, to enact laws, regulations, and administrative arrangements, and to repeal existing laws, regulations, and administrative arrangements as it deems necessary."

"Short and to the point," said Forsythe. "As good parliamentary drafting should be."

"I can't say I understand," said Turner.

Forsythe grimaced. "I'm not sure how many people did," he said. "Basically, it meant that the government could do whatever it damn well wanted, without having to go through Parliament. The government moved the amendment, and it was accepted, and the Meteorological Research Funding Bill passed through both chambers at 3.52am. Hardly any debate. Who really wants to argue about money for weather research, eh? The Governor-General signed it an hour later, to be effective immediately. The government made a Declaration under section 47A(ii) the next day.

"Then I helped the Emergency Council draw up a list of new laws. It was a long list. And then there was list of old laws that would be abolished. That was even longer. The election laws were the first to go."

Forsythe was silent for a long while. Then he said: "You have to realise that this was all legal. It's not like there was a coup or anything. Whether the members of Parliament who voted for it knew what they were doing is beside the point. The fact is that they did it, gave the government the power."

"If you say so," said Turner. "Nice and legal."

"Parliament actually continued on for a while after the Declaration. Passing resolutions and making speeches. But that was all they could do, talk," said Forsythe. "After the Council brought in the Media Freedom Act, so that all the journalists effectively worked for the government, even that was pointless, no-one got to hear them.

"But do you know the most ironic part? After a while, the Council realised that they didn't need public servants like me to draft complicated pieces of legislation any more. They could do it themselves, with their inner circle of advisers, keep everything simple and clear, allow the Green Corps as much discretion as they wanted when it came to implementation. So one day I received a letter saying that my whole office was 'unnecessary to the practical requirements of the existing circumstances'. Nice selection of language, don't you think? And it was made clear to me that I was no longer welcome in Canberra.

"So I took as many of the files as I could carry and left. I don't know why I took them, really. I suppose I thought there should be some sort of record of it, of the Declaration and all the other things that I worked on. Even having them is probably an offence."

Forsythe fell silent for a while. Then he said: "If I hadn't done it, hadn't drafted section 47A(ii), someone else would have. Maybe Corby herself, or some of the people around her, perhaps even de Silva, he was always involved in everything. But I was a public servant doing what a duly constituted government told me to do. I was following orders."

It sounded, thought Turner, like something that Forsythe had said many times. To himself, most likely.

"I was just following orders," Forsythe repeated.

"As we all do, usually," said Turner.

Forsythe shuffled through the papers again, pointlessly, his mind in another place, another time.

"And now," said Turner, looking around at the pathetic box, "you live in a shipping container."

"Yes," said Forsythe. "For my sins."

"Do you really think," said Turner, "that this somehow makes up for it?"

Forsythe stared at the folder in his hands. Section 47A(ii) of the Meteorological Research Funding Act. "No," he said eventually. "No, I don't think it does. Not even close. Never will."

The rain had stopped. It had only been a shower.

Turner watched the last few drops drift earthwards.

"I suppose it's what they depend on," he said. "What they have always depended on. That we wouldn't pay attention. That we would go along, because that was the easiest thing to do. That we would follow orders. One step at a time. Never look to see the whole picture. That we would stay silent."

Forsythe nodded. "I suppose so," he said. "One step at a time. Piece here, piece there. Until it was all gone. Until it was all lost."

Turner pushed his bike out of the shipping container, heading back towards the highway.

"Thanks for the shelter," he said.

"Thanks for the apple," said Forsythe. "And … I'm sorry."

"I know," said Turner. "But being sorry doesn't change anything."

Then he left Forsythe, with his papers and his files and his fathomless regret, behind, and he did not look back.

34. Tide

Pocka-pocka-pocka.

It's drawing me on, thought Turner. *Pulling me.*

If someone had asked him why he was going there, what he hoped to achieve, he doubted that he would be able to give an answer. Because there wasn't one, not really.

He remembered that when he had been a kid at the beach he would stand in the water, chest-deep, and feel the surge of the tide. The steady and certain drag of it. The will. There was no reason for it going in or out, it just did what it did, was what it was.

And now the tide was taking him south, relentlessly, constantly. It grew stronger as he moved closer. He often rode through the night, now, stopping for rest only when his aching body demanded it.

He looked down the empty road. *Pocka-pocka-pocka,* said the wheels of the bike.

The highway was the line of a tattoo, drawn over the veins and arteries beneath the surface. Over the pumping blood. Over the quiet flesh of the land.

The kilometres unfolded before him, and vanished behind him, sweeping over the horizon and away forever.

35. Cherokee

It was a Green Corps vehicle, an old Cherokee by the look of it, stopped across the highway, a simple but effective roadblock. As Turner came closer, he could see three GC members, two men and a woman, standing next to it. They all had batons in holsters on their belts. Not far away was a rusty, peeling sign, NOW ENTERING THE AUSTRALIAN CAPITAL TERRITORY.

Turner stopped, dismounted. He waited for them to speak.

"This is a stop-and-search," said the leader of the group, one of the men. "By the authority of the Prime Minister and the Emergency Council. Empty your pack and your pockets, and disclose your reasons for being on this road."

Turner scratched the stubble on his neck. "Stop and search, eh?" he said. "You know, you probably don't want to try either of those."

The man stared at him. Turner stared straight back.

"This one is a troublemaker," said the other GC guy.

Turner glanced at him. Then he lifted his sleeve to show his mark. "You know what this means?" he said. "That I really don't like people like you. That I've had enough of you. All of you. So get out of my way. Now."

The three of them continued to stare at him. Clearly, they were not used to this sort of thing. They expected respect, deference, obedience. They felt they deserved it.

But they were not ones to back down, either. The leader pulled his baton from its holster and swung at Turner.

But Turner was ready for it. Old instincts, from bar fights and police training, took over. He caught the man's arm and twisted it behind him, swivelling, wrenching the baton from his grip. He pushed the man down onto the hood of the Cherokee, face first. There was a crunch, and a sudden explosion of blood over the vehicle. Turner grabbed the man by the back of the neck, pulled him up, and smashed his face down again. And then again.

The second one was coming at him, baton raised. Turner lifted the club he was holding to block the blow, and then punched with his free hand, put all his weight into it, slamming into the man's gut. He gave a rasping cry and staggered backwards. Before he could recover, Turner hit him on the side of the head with the baton, and then again, other side. There was the sound of bones breaking, and a splash of dark blood from the man's temple. He went down.

The woman kicked out at him, some sort of fancy kung fu move. Turner took the blow on his side and grabbed the woman's ankle, wrapping his arm around it, pinning her. He smashed the baton onto her knee with as much force as he could muster. She screamed in pain as the joint shattered. Still holding her, he hit her across the face with the baton, and there was a gush of blood.

He flung her aside, and turned again to face the leader, who was struggling to get up, trying to use the Cherokee for support. Blood streamed from his splintered nose, from his mouth where the teeth had been.

Turner brought the baton down on the man's shoulder. He shouted as his collar-bone broke.

Turner looked around. All three of them were down, the two men unconscious or close enough to it. The woman was crawling, aimlessly, pointlessly, in shock, dragging her ruined leg behind her. Blood flowed from her face where the cheekbone was smashed.

He went to the Cherokee and opened the door. The keys were still in the ignition. He pulled them out and threw them as far as he could into the bush. He collected the batons and threw them away as well.

He walked over to the woman. He realised that she was young, maybe 25, maybe less. She might have been pretty. She would not be pretty again. He felt no sympathy for her.

"I told you not to try and stop me," he said.

She looked up at him, her eyes glazed with pain.

"Now what?" she gasped.

"Now," he said, "you can walk home."

He went back to his bike and got onto it, and rode away. In the distance, he thought he could see the hills of Canberra.

36. Ingenious

We are a tough, ingenious people, we Australians, thought Turner. We're good at solving the problems on our doorstep. Maybe that's why we let bad things happen sometimes, because we think we can fix them later. And if we decide it's going to be too hard to fix, then sometimes we vote with our feet.

He didn't blame people for leaving, going overseas, wherever they could get to. And he didn't blame those who were left for turning inwards, looking to local problems and immediate solutions, doing their best to not see the country's story.

We are a people forever poised between the desert and the beach, he thought. Between doing it tough and taking it easy. In adversity, we pull together. We don't turn on each other, not usually, not most of us. You have to admire that, it might be our finest quality. But the other side of it is that we let too much pass, too much go by, things are lost before we realise it, things that might have been saved if we had …

Our tragedy, he said silently to himself, *is that we are too quick to forget.*

37. Cost

He threw down the shotgun. He turned to the Green Corps squad leader.

"This isn't right," he said. "These people haven't done anything wrong. They haven't done anything."

He looked at the little crowd. Battered, exhausted. They'd come a long way, and all they had to show for it was the dust of the road.

Turner looked up at the sculptures on the front of the building, figures in a triangular frame at the top. He looked again at the people in front of him.

The Green Corps leader raised his arm, about to give the signal. Turner heard the bolt of the heavy machine gun on the truck slide into place, ready, locking the ammunition belt into the firing position. He heard a dozen shotgun safety catches click off.

"You can't do this!" shouted Turner. "It isn't right!"

"What's right," said the GC leader, "is what I say is right. And what is needed here is a lesson. I have the authority to provide that."

Turner punched him, once, twice, knocking him down.

The guy got to his feet. He rubbed his jaw, spat out a mouthful of blood. He smiled, knowing that the punches had meant nothing, less than nothing. "That will cost you," he said. "A Recal mark and ten years behind wire. If you are lucky."

Turner raised his fist to hit the man again. And then he saw, from the corner of his eye, the spark of a taser, in the hands of another GC member. It struck him in the back.

He went down, convulsing, onto the concrete. Vaguely, almost as if it was in the distance, he heard the machine gun and the shotguns open up.

If I had acted earlier, he thought. *If I had done something else. If I had done something —*

38. Alone

If I had done something, I might have saved them, he thought.

The spike of Black Mountain Tower, rising up from a mountain covered in bush, was on his right. Once it had provided telecommunication services for the city. Now it was inhabited mainly by feral animals, by the look of it.

The Australian War Memorial was on his left, tucked back in the shadow of a hill. No, it was called the International Victims Monument now, that was one of the changes brought in after the Declaration. Whatever, he said to himself. Symbolic things didn't matter much now.

If I had done something ...

His muscles were knots of pain, and the bike rattled and creaked.

He was almost at the lake when the bike collapsed under him, sending him sprawling onto the asphalt. He got up, examined the broken frame, the bald tyres.

"Thanks for getting me this far," he said softly. "I guess I have to go on alone from here."

He hefted his pack onto his back and started across the bridge, forcing himself to walk slowly. No rush, he thought, looking at the towering flagpole of Parliament House. Not like it's going anywhere.

And now I do something.

39. 7-millimetre

He walked up the concourse that led to Parliament House. He had been here before, many years ago. He was just a kid at the time, and it had been a trip with a school class. Looked very different then.

Once the concourse had been paved but now it looked as if many of the stones had been removed, and there were large patches of bare dirt and overgrown grass. There had been a sort of fountain as well, flowing gently down the slope. Now it was nothing more than a pool of stagnant water.

There was some activity around, it looked as if some of the public service offices nearby still had people working in them. There was a group of men with picks and shovels, digging up the underground irrigation system and putting the pipes onto the back of a wagon.

On the hill that covered the building, there were sheep and goats grazing, and there were little piles of animal excrement here and there on the concourse. The flag of the Republic moved slowly on its pole, drifting in the gusts of wind that came down from the heavy clouds. There was a bank of windmills; some were still turning.

He had expected that there would be security guards at the door. Metal detectors and x-ray machines, which could be a problem, given what was in his pack. But there was nothing, no guards, and the door themselves were broken, locked in an open position.

He went in, and walked slowly along the curved, silent hallway.

So these are the corridors of power, he thought. There was a pungent, acrid smell in the air. *Must be the sheep.*

Most of the offices he passed were dark and empty, but in a few there were people. They were sitting at desks and writing on computers or pieces of paper. God knows what they were doing. Or what they thought they were doing. There were still lights on, probably powered by the windmills he had seen.

He stopped and looked around. No-one. He took off his pack and reached into the compartment sewn into the bottom. He took the pistol out and put it into the pocket of his jacket. Glock 7-millimetre, police issue, dead reliable. Six bullets in the clip. *No*, he thought, *only five. Dyson*. Well, five would be enough.

He looked at his hands. The dirt seemed to have got under his skin, worked its way into the pores, become a part of him. The dust of the road, 1200 kilometres of it. Grey. Brown. Red.

He had thought that he might be scared when he got here. He thought he might simply freeze, wondering what he should do now. But he felt immensely calm, sure of himself, ready to do what he had come to do.

Do something right.

The weight of the gun was almost a comfort.

As he moved deeper into the building the signs of decay increased. The carpet, once green, was stained, worn through in places. Some of the office doors swung loose on broken hinges, and occasionally there was faded, indecipherable graffiti on the walls.

Eventually, he came to a desk. There was a man in a faded uniform sitting there. His shirt said Security. He was playing a card game on an ancient computer. He looked up when Turner approached.

"Hi," he said. "Are you here for the tour?" A joke, presumably.

"No," said Turner. "I am here to see the Prime Minister."

Security grunted.

"What for?" he said.

Turner said nothing. In his pocket, he put his hand on the butt of the Glock. He eased the safety catch off.

Security grunted again. Then he pointed along the corridor. "Third door on the left," he said. "Right after the Director's office."

40. RECAL

The Prime Minister of the Republic of Australia, Jonathan de Silva, was sitting at his desk, alone in his office. The desk was covered in books, open, showing glossy pages.

Turner took the gun from his pocket.

The Prime Minister looked up. He seemed … different … to his photographs. Older. Greyer. More gaunt.

If he saw the weapon in Turner's hand he gave no sign.

He said: "Hello."

Turner started a little, but said nothing.

"Are you here for an autograph?" said de Silva.

Turner shook his head.

De Silva gave a little nod and turned back to his books.

Turner picked up one of the volumes. It was called *The Wild Rivers of Tasmania*. It was full of beautiful pictures.

"Ah," said de Silva. "Did you bring me a new book? Many people do."

Turner handed *The Wild Rivers of Tasmania* to him. De Silva took it and looked at the cover.

"Ah, this one, I already have this one," he said. "But thank you anyway. It's wonderful, you see?" He showed a picture of cascading rapids, all silver and mist, to Turner.

Turner said nothing.

"We can save them," said de Silva. "We can save them. All of them. We have to."

"Do you know," said Turner, "that out there they are tattooing eight-year-old children?"

"Who is?"

"The Green Corps."

"Ah, the Green Corps. Good men and women. Most of them are young. Some are just teenagers. But committed. To the cause. To the environment."

Turner sat down on a chair across the desk to de Silva. He ran his fingers through his hair.

Then he lifted the gun and pointed it at de Silva.

De Silva opened another book and began to leaf through the pages. It was about the Daintree.

Turner watched the Prime Minister study the book, slowly turning the pages. The gun felt heavy in his hand.

Then Turner gave a sigh of resignation. He put the gun down on the desk.

Guess I'm not a killer, he thought. *I wasn't before, and I'm not now.*

"Have you been there?" said de Silva. "To north Queensland?"

"Can't say I have," said Turner.

"It's beautiful," said de Silva. "Beautiful."

"I'm sure it is," said Turner.

De Silva turned the book to again display the pictures, putting it on top of the gun.

Turner heard someone else come into the room, behind him. He stood up and turned around.

"He has good days and bad days," said Director Corby.

"And is this a good day or a bad day?" said Turner to her.

"Depends on how you think about it," she said. "You look like a man who has covered some ground."

"Enough to be able to tell you that the crisis is over," he said. "The climate is the same as ever. Sun, rain, all the rest. Good or bad as it has ever been. So you can tell the Green Corps to ease off. No more Emergency."

She stared at him, as if considering her next move in a game she had already won. Then she said: "Come with me."

She led Turner into her office, next to de Silva's. She took a document from the bookcase and handed it to him.

"This is the last copy of this in Australia," she said. "The others have all been destroyed. Burned, mainly, which you may think a bit odd. But it gets cold around here in the winter, let me tell you."

Turner looked at the cover of the book. It was a publication from a UN agency, one that had produced a string of reports. He remembered that at the farm this organisation had been one of the supervisors' favourites. In one lecture, a supervisor had described it as the source code for all that had followed. At the time, Turner had not really understood what that had meant. Now he understood.

But on the farm there had only been reports that were old, ones that had been published before 2012. The one in Turner's hands was titled Final Report. It was dated several years ago.

There was a bookmark in it, and he opened it there. It was the Executive Summary. One paragraph had been underlined by hand. It said: *The hiatus in global temperature rises first identified by this Panel seventeen years ago, in 2013, and at that time dating back for more than a decade, now appears to be permanent, aside from natural variability. While*

*the Panel cannot readily explain this, the statistical and observational evidence
is difficult to refute …*

Another paragraph: *Sea levels have shown some volatility but when
considered in detail they appear to be within the range of natural shifts.
However, definitive measurement has proved difficult as the observed rises have
been in centimetres rather than the metres previously predicted …*

Another: *While many policy actions to reduce greenhouse gas emissions,
sometimes very radical actions, have been taken over the past decade, there is
no clear evidence to show that they have had any impact on, or are the cause of,
the pause in temperature rises. It may, indeed, be the case that this Panel made
a significant misjudgement in relation to its initial assumptions …*

Turner closed the book. He did not understand all of it but he
could read the basic message. He looked at Corby.

She was smiling. An ironic smile.

"You … know?" said Turner. "Then you've known for years,
ever since this was published."

She nodded. "And I suspected for a long while before that,"
she said. "I spend some of my time travelling around the country,
you know, as much as conditions allow. I like to stay in touch. And
I get reports from the Green Corps as well. They're people that
I appointed, after all, most of them, and they know where their
loyalty lies. Their real loyalty."

"Then you'll know that a lot of people are doing it tough,"
said Turner. "Those who are left. Just scratching by with food and
other resources. Living off the bits and pieces of what there was
before. Not much electricity, almost no medicine, just the most
essential things of life in most cases, sometimes not even that.
Drinking bore and river water, worried about getting sick, scared
that the Green Corps will come knocking."

Corby gave an indifferent shrug. "You might see it that way," she said. "I see it as self-sufficient communities conserving scarce resources. And if some people fall by the wayside, well, that's just the cost of getting to where we want to go."

Turner stared at her, almost unbelieving. "So you consider all this to be a success?" he said. "This is what you intended? Carts and candles, rules and rot?"

"I consider it to be a necessary step," said Corby. "And we are almost ready for the next stage. For that, I have personally been conducting negotiations with some overseas friends."

"I didn't think we had any overseas friends," said Turner. "I thought you had BDSed them all."

"Not all of them," said Corby. "Not the Koreans."

"The South Koreans?" said Turner, surprised.

"No, the other ones," said Corby. "They'll get the place running again. They know how to get things into shape. Maybe they're the only ones who do, since all the others have apparently forgotten how to read the signs of history. And if you're worried about a shortage of electricity, I can tell you that we'll soon have plenty."

"Hard to see how, since you dismantled all the power stations," said Turner.

Corby pointed to a map of Australia on the wall. "I'm not talking about coal or gas or wind or solar," she said. "I'm talking about hydro. Plenty of sites available. There are even cases, some going back a couple of decades, where blueprints were drawn up but the project didn't proceed. Our friends will be able to use those plans to start construction immediately. Get industry moving again. The right sort of industry, this time, with the right rules. Take the eco out of eco-socialism."

Turner looked at the map. Coloured pins indicated the proposed sites. Tasmania, the Western Australian coast, north Queensland. There were many pins.

Corby moved around to the other side of her desk. She picked up a pencil and tapped it on some papers. "If there is nothing more I can do for you," she said to Turner, "perhaps you should be on your way."

"No," said a voice from the doorway. It was de Silva. He came into the office, staring at Corby. He obviously had been listening. "We have to protect the rivers," he said. "The wild rivers. And the forests. From development. We have to ensure that they're safe. We can do it. For future generations."

"Humph," said Corby. "Screw the wild rivers and fuck the forests. Go back to your picture books, you stupid old man. We don't need you anymore."

Slowly, wordlessly, De Silva raised his arm. He was holding Turner's gun.

He fired, twice. The bullets hit Corby in the chest.

Seven-millimetre.

The impact threw Corby backwards into her chair. She gasped in astonishment. Then she looked down at her chest, at the spreading red stain.

She looked at Turner. "Who *are* you!?" she said.

"Just a guy," said Turner. He lifted his sleeve to show the tattoo. "Just another Recal."

Corby touched the blood pumping out of her. She examined her red fingers, as if they belonged to someone else.

"But," she said softly, almost to herself, "we were building a whole new world ... I was so close ... "

She coughed once, spluttered. Her eyes closed. That was it.

The security guard who had been on the desk outside came running in. He saw Corby dead in her chair, saw de Silva with the Glock still smoking in his hand.

He looked at Turner. Turner shrugged. There was nothing to say.

Security nodded slightly. Then he backed out of the room, into the corridor. There was the sound of him walking away.

De Silva held out the gun to Turner. "This is yours," he said. "You left it in my office. I came in here to give it back to you. But then – " he gestured towards Corby.

"Tell you what," said Turner. "You keep it. You're obviously better at using it than I am. And, who knows, you might need it."

"Really?" said de Silva. "Well, thank you, thank you very much." He turned to stare at Corby. Turner wondered if the Prime Minster understood what he had done. He wondered if he cared.

He thought about the tide, about how it changed direction, inevitably, about how it felt on the skin of a boy.

He had a feeling that he wouldn't have any more bad dreams.

41. North

He left the office and walked along the hallway. He reached the desk.

Security was taking thick pads of paper and boxes of pencils from a cupboard and putting them into a bag. He saw Turner watching him.

"Damned if I'm leaving here with nothing," he said. "And these things are really valuable."

The last pad would not fit into his bag. He offered it to Turner. "Think you can use this?" he said.

"Yeah, maybe I can," said Turner. He took it and put it into his pack.

The two of them walked along the corridor. They went through the broken doors of the Parliament House of the Republic of Australia and stood on the concrete roadway that ran around the complex. Before them, there were lines of overgrown trees, and, beyond that, low grasslands, and on the horizon were lines of mountains, mottled grey rolling into purple.

Turner felt the breeze on his face. He could hear a bird, somewhere, and the faint hum of a wind turbine. The sky, overcast before, had become a cerulean blue.

"I'm going that way," said Security, gesturing along the road. "How about you?"

Turner nodded in the other direction.

"What are you going to do, now?" said Security.

Turner was quiet for a long moment. Then he said: "Keep doing what I've been doing, I guess. Travel around. Listen to people's stories, write them down. I think I might head north. There's a woman there I'd like to see again." He smiled at the thought of her.

"What about that?" said Security, pointing at the tattoo on Turner's arm. "You goin' to have it removed?"

Turner looked at it. RECAL.

"Maybe not removed," he said. "Maybe amended. Put an I at the front and an L at the end."

"Huh," said Security. "Well, it's your skin." He hefted the bag of stolen paper. "Guess I'll see you," he said.

"Yeah, maybe," said Turner.

He watched Security walk away, until he turned a corner and was out of sight.

He adjusted his pack. It was lighter, without the gun.

He went down a flight of stone steps and through the trees and away from the big building, and away from the room where the dead woman and the man with his books were. He continued walking, and eventually the city vanished behind him, and the path became a road, and he was walking along it, a shaded road, a luminous road, a road that might have led nowhere, or might have led everywhere.

Derek Parker is a Melbourne-based freelance writer. His work appears in *Australian Spectator, the Financial Review, the Australian, In the Black* and *American Review.* He is the author of a non-fiction book, *The Courtesans: The Press Gallery in the Hawke Era.* He does not have a blog. He is not on Facebook. He does not tweet.

www.ingramcontent.com/pod-product-compliance
Lightning Source LLC
Chambersburg PA
CBHW051839020726
47502CB00005B/1863